Table of Contents

Chapter One

So, a blind chick walks into a bar looking for a supervillain.

Sounds like the setup to a bad joke, right?

Just wait.

Face recognition pinged Red Cypher at this infested rat hole an hour ago. I'd paid through the nose for a cabby to ignore the suggested speed limit and get me here before the cybercriminal was once more in the wind.

The bar was loud, but not with conversation. Laughter, too sharp to be friendly, voices shouting obscenities, tangled together with the low thrum of bass-heavy music, which made the air hum against my skin.

I took a slow breath, the air tasting of old beer and fried grease that had been used one too many times. Somewhere to my left, a ceiling fan groaned in protest with every turn, pushing the stale air in lazy circles.

I moved towards the bar, the long counter a dark shadow in my vision. I could make out the bartender, a broad, heavyset man who caused the floorboards to creak with every step.

Conversation stilled as I made my way in, white cane tapping steadily. The hush wasn't polite. It was the kind of pause predators make when something unfamiliar walks into their territory. Perhaps I should've changed out of the smart pantsuit I'd worn to work.

"Sweetheart," a voice said to my right, close enough that I could smell the liquor on their breath. "I hate to tell you, but you're definitely in the wrong place."

I ignored them and straightened my back.

"I'm looking for Red Cypher," I declared to the room at large.

The silence sharpened, then cracked with a low, mocking laugh from somewhere in the back.

"Yeah," said the same voice as before. "You're definitely in the wrong place. Nut house is two blocks back—" A hand closed around my wrist.

With a sharp flick, I broke his hold and slammed my cane into his gut.

"Don't touch me," I growled, heart pounding with anxiety. I could feel the eyes of every person laser-focused on me. A million sharp pin pricks stabbing across my skin.

The man groaned. "That was a fucking mistake, you little—"

"Sit back down, Hazard." A voice said from just behind me. I jumped in surprise and spun around. The person was dressed all in red, the colour bright and sharp in my limited line of sight.

"Fine, she can be your fucking problem then, Cypher," Hazard growled, his voice growing distant as he stomped away.

"What are you all staring at?" Red Cypher demanded. "Go back to your knitting."

He didn't wait to see if they'd comply, simply taking my arm and leading me roughly to the far end of the bar.

"Balls of steel on you, little girl," he said to me when we stopped. He took a seat at the bar, the stool sliding noisily against the floor. He smelt of stale coffee and burnt metal, like the smoke off a soldering iron. "Your luck is about to wear out. I suggest you piss off while you still can."

"I need to talk to you," I said.

"Then talk," he insisted. "Lou! Another whiskey sour."

I swallowed, nerves buzzing under my skin as I pulled a card from my pocket and set it on the bar. "My name is Velvet Walker. I'm an attorney employed by the Miracle Network. I wanted to reach out because there's a boy at St. Mercy hospital whose last request is to meet..."

"This is a joke, right?" Red Cypher interrupted. "I don't know what you think you're doing, but you are playing with fire, Ms. Walker."

"Yes, I mean no. This isn't a joke." I hurried to explain. I fumbled the file from my bag. "This is Charlie Glynn. He's fifteen and has a brain tumour. He's been teaching himself coding, and you're his role model."

Red Cypher turned to look at me, his face a shadowy haze beneath his red cowl. "Go back to the Super Alliance and tell them that they'll have to do better than a sob story and a pretty face. Black Bullet is really off his game."

Stress, sleeplessness, embarrassment and the insinuation that I might be just a stupid pawn of that smug bastard Black Bullet, broke me.

Tears burned down my face, and I stomped my foot like a child. "Will you shut up and listen to me? This boy has months to live, and for some bizarre reason, the only thing he wants is to meet your smug ass. I haven't been surveilling this shitty bar for the last two weeks so that you could accuse me of being some super's stooge! If you have even a shred of self-respect, you would at least consider this."

The bar had gone silent again, every eye burrowing into us. The floor creaked, and there was a dull thud as the bartender put Red Cypher's drink onto the counter. The glass clinked in his hand as Red Cypher lifted it to his lips and downed it in a single swallow. Paper crinkled in his hand, while he gathered up my card and Charlie's file, before taking my arm and dragging me out behind the bar into the back alleyway.

Yup, this is it. I thought. *This is how I die. They'll write it on my tombstone. Here lies Velvet Walker, the idiot who yelled at a supervillain in the middle of a crowded bar.*

"I'm sorry, I'm sorry," I mumbled as I pulled myself away from the light of the doorway, the little vision I had now completely obscured. "I didn't mean...I...I..."

He came to an abrupt halt, dropping my arm and flipping briefly through the file. A computerized beep emanated from his suit. "Charlie Glynn, St. Mercy Hospital. Room 338, MRI with contrast reveals a 3.5 cm mass located in the left parietal lobe. Fuck that's rough."

I tried to orient myself towards the sound of his voice, confused.

"Er..."

"That was a really dangerous move you just made," he said to me. "Do you know how many criminals were in that bar? At least eight murderers and two suspected rapists, and you waltz in there with your leather bag and designer loafers and act like you're invincible."

My toes curled in my shoes. "I got these on sale—"

"This isn't a trick?" he cut me off. "You legitimately tracked me down to fulfill this boy's last wish?"

"Y, yes," I confirmed, still unsure as to whether I would actually survive this encounter.

Red Cypher sighed. "I can't promise anything."

I gaped in shock. "You mean--?"

"I'm not promising anything," he repeated. "Any sign of supes or cops and it'll be your neck I wring."

"Trust me," I insisted. "I don't want to involve the police any more than you do. I wasn't even supposed to come, but I couldn't get a hold of anyone else, and I didn't know how long you'd be here..."

There was silence, and my face grew warm at the feel of Red Cypher's penetrating gaze on me, the hairs on my neck standing on end.

He shifted, a crinkle of paper and the rustle of fabric. I jumped at the sound of a cable unspooling into the night, a noise like a zipline flying upward, and I found myself alone in the dark alleyway.

My knees gave out, and I collapsed to the ground, mud soaking my pants as I hyperventilated. My nails dug into the loose gravel as I worked through my panic, struggling to get my racing heart back in control.

It was a long time before I was able to pick myself back up and make my way to the public street. Ignoring the catcalling of the barflies, I stumbled over to the nearest street lamp and used my phone to summon another cab. As I waited and the adrenaline of the situation faded, I found myself agreeing with Red Cypher, this had been a very stupid idea.

My cane tapped rhythmically against the pavement as I made my way up the drive of the small condo I shared with my mother. I prayed that she, at least, had remained asleep during my outing. Lord knows what she would have done if she knew.

The door was unlocked, pushing open easily under my hand. My pulse jumped into my throat as I took in the strange, empty silence of the house.

My mother's presence was full and vibrant at best, overwhelming and suffocating at worst, but it was always there, even in sleep. Her soft snores because she refused to get treated for her sleep apnea, her humming as she made tea or the scratch of a pen on paper as she made notes. Tonight, there was nothing, only the low creak of the floorboards under my shoes and the soft tap-tap of my cane.

"Mom?" My voice fell flat against the dark.

The kitchen smelled sharp, wrong. The tang of bleach cut over the usual herbs and dust. My hand brushed something on the floor, a dropped glass, maybe? I bent, fingers grazing the surface. A needle.

I jolted forward, arm stretched out in front of me as I followed the smell, the silence pressing down harder the farther I went. My hand skimmed the wall until I reached the doorframe of her study.

She was there, prone on the ground, the outline of her body against the faint glow of the desk lamp, slumped unnaturally, head tilted at an awkward angle.

The cane clattered from my hand as I stumbled forward. I dropped to my knees beside her. "Mom! Mom, wake up!" My hands shook as I struggled to pull her into my arms while simultaneously dialling nine-one-one.

"1003 Henigmen Place," I blurted frantically into the receiver. "Sixty-six-year-old woman unresponsive, suspected drug overdose."

I ran my fingers over her face, her neck, desperately searching for a pulse.

And then it hit me.

The rush, the flood of my odd sixth sense. A map of chemicals, molecules and patterns seared into my awareness. My mother's DNA was familiar, a lullaby I'd known since birth. But tangled into it, clinging to her clothes and hair, was something foreign. A second pattern, jagged, heavy and undeniable.

"Someone else was here," I said into the phone, interrupting the operator.

"What was that?" the operator asked. "The ambulance is on the way."

"Someone else was here," I said with absolute certainty. "Someone killed my mother."

"Ma'am, just hang on," the operator urged. "Help is on the way."

I wrapped my arms around my mother's cold body and gripped her close, knowing that help was already much too late.

Chapter Two

The police didn't put much weight into my murder theory. Though they did agree to have forensics look into it.

"This isn't the first time your mother overdosed," The officer in charge of my mother's case reminded me.

"That was a year ago," I told him. "She's been clean for six months."

"Relapses are very common." His pitying tone was infuriating.

"The door was open when I got home," I told him. "Someone else had been in the house."

"Are you sure you shut it properly when you left?" My boss Georgie asked, during a visit a few days later, after I'd recounted the story to her.

"I'm sure I did."

"Where did you go anyway? It's not like you to run out at two in the morning."

At that question, I went silent.

Mentioning my meeting with Red Cypher would only make a bad situation even more complicated. I didn't want the hassle while I went through the motions of getting my mother's affairs in order and organizing a funeral. Of course, the other, more selfish reason was, I didn't want it getting back to Charlie. Charlie, who at best only had a few months left. Despite his words, I couldn't make myself believe that Red Cypher would show up. Charlie would be devastated, and I just didn't have the strength to let another kid down.

Two weeks passed, and I found myself slowly losing my mind. The house, my life, the entire world was, at the same time, completely hollow and also too much. People and things and noises, crowding all around me, while also somehow feeling utterly meaningless in this hellish new normal.

I left the house and boarded the bus to the office with the singular purpose of demanding to come back to work, even if just part-time. The bus smelled faintly of coffee and diesel, with the sour tang of damp coats pressed too close together. I sat near the middle, cane balanced against my leg, fingers curled tight around the strap of my bag. The world outside was nothing but a grey blur, intercut with blinding patches of morning light, enough to make my head ache.

Even amongst the familiar routine, the seat beneath me felt alien, as though the ground could drop away at any moment.

Three blocks away from work, the bus made an abrupt screeching halt. My shoulders slammed back into the seat. Gasps and shouts followed, then the collective hush of held breath.

Outside, the sound of destruction rolled like thunder. Metal crumbling, concrete shattering. Explosions cracked through the morning air.

"Holy shit, it's Black Bullet!" Someone said from over my shoulder. "He's fighting Shockwave!"

The bus erupted into chatter, half a dozen voices pressed up against the windows, narrating every blast and strike. Phones clicked and chimed as people scrambled to capture the moment.

"He's got him pinned down by the bridge!"

"Ouch! He looks stunned. No, he's getting back up! Go Black Bullet!"

I pinched the bridge of my nose, irritated and impatient. The hero worship was louder than the fight itself. They didn't care about the screams or the ambulances struggling to get through the chaos. All they cared about was their golden boy in spandex.

The battle dragged on. Bursts of energy, cheers each time the "right" man landed a blow. Then, suddenly, a different kind of silence. Expectant.

The bus doors hissed open. Heavy boots climbed the steps, sure and confident. A ripple of excitement swept through the passengers, whispers tumbling over one another.

"Black Bullet!" Someone gasped.

"I can't believe he's here!"

"Black Bullet, can we get a picture?" Someone asked.

"Of course you can!" The voice was jovial and smooth. Phone cameras clicked. "Is everyone alright?"

There was a general chorus of agreement with Black Bullet praising them all for their bravery and how they were the true heroes—such bullshit.

"Velvet Walker?" Black Bullet called out, and I would've been less surprised if he'd punched me in the face. "What a happy coincidence, just the person I wanted to see."

I kept my face blank. My eyes fixed on nothing, though my grip on my cane betrayed me. His footsteps moved closer, unhurried, until the scent of ozone and leather filled my nose.

"Ms. Walker," he said and though his tone was casual, there was a weight to it. "I was hoping we could have a word. Please, would you join me for a cup of coffee?"

I swallowed, hyper aware of every eye fixated on the two of us. "—I'm going to be late for work."

"Oh, I'm sure they'll understand." He reached out and took my arm, tugging me from my seat with a firm grip. "This way."

I jerked my arm out of his grip, something that would have been impossible if he'd been at all trying to hold on. "I can manage."

The crowd made way for us, making it easy to pick my way through the bus and down the stairs. Black Bullet directed me towards a nearby coffee shop. My cane kept catching on random bits of debris and long cracks in the sidewalk. The air still reeked of ozone and burning concrete. Sirens wailed faintly in the distance. When we entered the café, two workers had to take a moment to find some unbroken chairs for our table.

"So," Black Bullet began, the heavy fabric of his cape rustling as he sat. Static crackled around him, the iron scent of scorched metal lingering on his skin. "I was very surprised when I saw the news this morning."

"You'll have to enlighten me," I told him, voice flat.

"Charlie Glynn?" His tone carried the smug patience of a man lecturing a child. "The terminal case you were in charge of? Red Cypher made a point of visiting him. Strange, isn't it? A man who hacked into the city's servers and shut down all police communication for two days suddenly wants to play philanthropist?"

I took a breath, uncertain if I should answer truthfully, while knowing full well that lying would be useless. "We did inform Titan Global that a child had requested a visit from a supervillain."

"And the Super Alliance was willing to make that happen, under preapproved circumstances." Black Bullet reminded me. "We were supposed to be kept in the loop.

"I realize that, and I was going to let you know, but the same day I met with Red Cypher," I paused, swallowing down tears. "Something else came up."

"Something else?" Black Bullet asked, impatient. "That kept you occupied for two weeks?"

"My mother was murdered," I spat at him. "So, yes, I've been a bit busy."

Black Bullet paused, and because his back was to the sun, it was impossible to make out his expression. "Who was your mother?" He asked, finally.

"Dr. Morag Walker," I told him. "She was a chemistry professor at the University. Former chemistry professor."

"Right." Black Bullet said slowly. "I remember that case. I thought it was deemed a suicide."

"Agree to disagree," I spat, bitterly, completely done with this whole conversation. "What exactly do you want from me? You didn't pull me off that bus just to ask about my family."

"No," Black Bullet said sharply. "No, I wanted to talk about Red Cypher. We're going to need you to get in contact with him again—"

I stood from the table, my cane knocking against the top and causing it to tilt dangerously. "We're done here."

"We absolutely are not," Black Bullet protested. "You've been in contact with a wanted criminal."

"One time, at a bar," I told him. "As an attorney, I can tell you, you'd need a lot more than that to convince a judge I've done anything wrong, but please go ahead, I could use the distraction." I unfolded my cane and turned to go.

Black Bullet stood from the table, his chair toppling to the debris-covered floor. "You don't understand what you've invited into your life. Red Cypher, just like all villains, doesn't do kindness. Not without reason. He's using that boy, just like he's using you."

I frowned. "You don't know that."

"I know more than you ever will," he said. "Men like him don't change. They just switch tactics. Find softer targets."

My throat burned as anger bled into fear. "If you're so sure, why not have one of your lackeys take him out already?"

That made him chuckle, though the sound held no humour. "Because I don't clean up small messes. I crush threats. Red Cypher is circling the drain. The question is whether he drags you down with him."

I heard the snap of static when he flexed his hand. The smell of ozone again, sharp and electric. He didn't need to touch me for me to feel the weight of the warning.

And then he was gone, boots ringing steadily against the broken pavement, the crowd roaring his name as though he hadn't just threatened a defenseless blind woman.

"Hey, Black Bullet," I called after him. His footsteps were fading fast, and for a moment I wondered if he'd heard me.

"Yes?" he called back, hopeful.

"I'll make you a deal," I said, voice carrying over the rising crowd, echoing through the ruined buildings. "I'll help you track down Red Cypher if you can tell me who Samuel Hall is."

A beat and then. "Who?"

I let out a slow breath, nodding to myself. "That's what I thought." I turned and walked away.

Chapter Three

The Miracle Network office was a warzone. Phones rang without pause, printers groaned and spluttered. The constant murmur of desperate voices spilled from every corner. Parents begging, pleading, demanding the same impossible thing. *My child also wants to meet a villain!*

My head throbbed from the noise. I wanted to sink into the carpet, let the whole building collapse over me, and let Titan Global sweep up the pieces.

"Velvet Walker?"

I turned towards the voice. Bright, sharp and slightly accented. The woman's hair was dyed a vibrant pink, making it easy for me to pick her out of the crowd.

"I'm Casey," she announced before I could respond. "You're new assistant. Georgie said you would be the one to stop me from lighting this place on fire, yes?"

"My assistant?" I repeated, dazed. Georgie had a bad habit of throwing people at me like sandbags when the dam burst.

"Yes, yes." With a muffled crash, a stack of files was dropped onto a nearby desk. "Phones are ringing off the hook. Georgie is crying in the bathroom, volunteers are useless. You? You are the one who brought the sky down on our heads. Now you will be the one to lift it again."

I blinked, trying to take her in. Her carefree attitude and the steel edge beneath her accent prickled under my skin. A phone rang nearby, and Casey answered with a curt, "Miracle Network, please don't yell at me," while scribbling notes with a speed that made my head spin.

For a moment, I just stood there, letting the storm of her energy buffer against me. Then I reached out for the nearest phone, because there wasn't time to question Georgie's judgment or my own unease.

Eventually, Georgie appeared to confront me herself. It was impossible to tell if she'd really been in the bathroom crying, but I decided it didn't matter as she lay into me about the upheaval I'd caused.

"A heads up, Velvet." She said, dropping into a nearby chair. "Just a little heads up is all I ask. Red Cypher walking into Charlie's room went viral overnight. Millions of views. Millions, Velvet." She leaned close enough that I could smell the coffee on her breath, sharp and bitter. She'd definitely gone with the extra espresso this morning.

"The Miracle Network isn't supposed to work like this. We're supposed to coordinate, vet, and control, these meetings. And now everyone wants a villain for their kid."

I leaned back in my chair, vinyl creaking. "According to Titan Global, villains don't do hospital visits."

"They do now," Georgie's laugh was tight, brittle. "Because apparently Red Cypher cares, or at least fakes in well enough for people to believe he does. Titan Global has already put out a press release. The court of popular opinion was a big deciding factor, I think. They want to support each child getting their wishes but cannot ensure the safety and well-being of all individuals involved."

I barked a laugh. "How very political of them."

"They're just covering their own ass," Georgie told me. "Just like we need to. Would a general waiver cover us legally?"

"Legally? Yes." I said. "Morally...?"

Georgie waved a hand. "With the way the donations are coming in, I can afford to lose a little sleep over morals."

A phone shrilled inches from my ear. Someone in the next cubicle snapped, "We don't coordinate that. No, ma'am, I don't care if your nephew likes pyrotechnics, Hazard Waste is not an option for a birthday party."

The absurdity would've been funny if it hadn't felt like the world was tilting under my feet. Red Cypher, Charlie, Black Bullet, appearing on the bus, my mother's blood cooling on the floor. It all pressed down like a collapsing ceiling.

"What do you want me to do?" I asked, my voice quieter than I meant it to.

Georgie exhaled, sharp and tired. "Keep doing what you always do, Velvet. Keep answering. Keep finding the loopholes. Keep making miracles. Because if we can't manage this, the Supes will. And you know what that means."

I did. Titan Global was just waiting for us to fail. To prove we were all wrong to ever trust a villain.

"Okay," I said.

Georgie clapped her hands together. "Great, first things first. You need to get back in touch with your new friend. We're going to need his help with all this."

"I have no idea how I'm going to do that, but I'll do my best," I said. "Who are we getting requests for?"

"Mistress Medea, Hazard Waste, Obsidian, Dark Omen... "Georgie recounted.

"Dark Omen, isn't he in prison?" I asked.

"Maybe we can make a deal for time served if he agrees to visit," Georgie mused. "And I know for a fact Emerald Shade is on parole. She might need community service hours."

"But what about all the others who would want to avoid going to jail," I asked. "Not all of these are non-violent criminals like Red Cypher. We have a duty to protect these kids."

Georgie waved a dismissive hand. "Like I said, talk to your friend, see who he thinks would play nice. The board of directors is willing to give you whatever you need to make this happen. Donations are already up ten percent, and they want to avoid any chance of you being head-hunted by another organization. This means a significant raise, Velvet."

I blinked, not certain how to respond. "Can I get a bigger office?" I asked after a beat.

"Done."

"With a window?"

"Absolutely."

I took a moment, not wanting to push my luck. "Is Casey really my assistant?"

"You are her only priority starting today."

"Okay," I replied, still completely off kilter. "Okay. I guess I'll go get started."

Georgie rose, the wheels on her chair squealing as they rolled across the carpet. "Let me know if there's anything else you need."

Casey was already moving my things into the vacant office on the second floor.

"You should have asked for an espresso machine!" She told me as she hauled boxes into the new space. "Or an ice cream maker."

I laughed. "Maybe after we start showing results. I don't even know how I'm going to get a hold of Red Cypher again. We'll have to start with the villains currently imprisoned or on parole. We'll need to contact the district attorney to arrange a deal."

"Your chair is ten steps to your right." Casey huffed and pulled off the lid to a box she'd just brought in. "Don't worry about Red Cypher, I already sent him a private message."

I miscounted and nearly fell on my butt trying to sit down. "You what?"

Casey blinked at me. "What? He has a Twitter account. I just said you needed to talk to him."

"When?" I squeaked, "Where?"

Casey snorted. "That's up to him, isn't it?"

I groaned. "And if he doesn't reach out?"

She made a noise of indifference. "We do what we can with what we've got."

I had no choice but to comply. The rest of the day was a whirlwind of phone calls and paperwork. Several families came to the office in person to inquire about a possible visit from a villain.

"I want to meet, Medea!" A little girl in a wheelchair proclaimed proudly. "She does magic."

Mistress Medea was a villain with a connection to otherworldly magic, able to conjure things from thin air, transport herself from place to place and project illusions at will. She was best known for her prankster nature. She would draw attention from her true goal by causing general chaos and mayhem.

Just last month, she absconded with every single pen from the downtown Royal

Bank, along with all the ink cartridges from every single printer. It wasn't until hours later that the manager realized they were also missing several kilograms of gold bars from the vault.

"She is pretty funny," I agreed with the little girl.

"Did you really go out and find Red Cypher?" her brother asked me.

I nodded. "It wasn't a very safe thing for me to do," I admitted.

"Do you have superpowers?" he asked.

I hesitated, then shook my head.

"I think you do," he told me. "I think your power is finding people."

"Maybe," I agreed before I was pulled away to take a phone call. It was Charlie's mother. Her voice was full of tears as she expressed her gratitude.

"I nearly had a heart attack this morning when we found a supervillain in Charlie's hospital room," she admitted. "But I don't remember the last time I saw him that happy. Red Cypher even upgraded Charlie's computer. The two of them rambled on about computers and technology for an hour. I didn't understand half of it, but he hasn't stopped smiling since."

I had to take a moment to wipe my eyes before replying. "I'm so glad," I told her, voice thick.

"We've been reading all the comments and articles. Are you getting more requests for kids to meet supervillains?"

"Yes," I said. "We're working on logistics."

"I know not everyone will like it, but if you can make other children as happy as you made Charlie, I think it will be worth it."

It was very late by the time Casey and I called it quits and decided to head home. I didn't like the idea of returning to the painfully empty house after such a busy, fulfilling day.

Despite my dread, my stomach growled. I felt ravenous for the first time in weeks. I stopped at the market next to the bus stop for a loaf of bread to go with some leftover stew. Distracted with the thought of supper and maybe going over some of my mother's files, I stepped into the house and flicked on the lights.

The sudden brightness overwhelmed my already limited sight, and as I paused in the doorway, the smell of coffee and soldering metal hit me full in the face.

I dropped my bag and clutched my cane in my hand like a baseball bat.

"Whose there?" I demanded, squinting into the room, my gaze settling on the vibrant red blur seated across the room.

"It's about time." Red Cypher said from his place on my sofa. "I expected you hours ago."

Chapter Four

I didn't scream. I wasn't even afraid. I simply lowered my cane and bent to pick up my discarded shopping bag.

"You could have called first," I complained, making my way towards the kitchen.

"You messaged me." He said, his footsteps just behind mine. "I took it as an invitation."

"To break into my house?" I asked, setting the bag on the counter and turning to face him, hands on my hips.

"I didn't think it wise to call on you during office hours. Especially after your impromptu appointment this morning."

I swallowed and lowered my head. "I didn't tell them anything."

"I know."

I blinked. "Did, did you bug the coffee shop?" I asked.

"The whole world is bugged," Red Cypher proclaimed. "I merely take advantage of the fact."

I frowned, but didn't make further comment as I turned back to the countertop.

"Would you like a drink?" I asked, reaching for the highest cupboard.

I flinched away as Red Cypher appeared at my side, his feet a bare whisper against the tile floor. "Let me help you."

I brushed his hand away, indignantly. "I know my way around my own kitchen," I told him, bringing down two glass tumblers and a bottle of whiskey. Using my thumb as a guide, I poured each of us a healthy measure, knocking mine back in one large swallow. I sighed at the comforting burn.

"Tough day?" Cypher asked, his own glass clinking against the countertop.

"Tough life," I replied, pouring a second glass.

"I'm sorry about your mother," he told me, voice soft. "I wanted to give you more time, after I heard, but Charlie's latest test results were less than optimal, and I thought it would be all right since you were planning to return to work."

"The world really is bugged. I only mentioned that to Georgie yesterday." I sipped my drink, slowly this time, as I gathered my thoughts. My throat was tight with tears. "Thank you for doing that. I—" I couldn't go on, slumping against the counter and sobbing over the loaf of bread. Strong gloved hands took my heaving shoulders and guided me across the room and onto the couch. A soft tissue was pushed into my hand.

I mopped at my wet face. The couch shifted beside me, and an arm wrapped around my shoulder. I pressed my face into the stiff fabric of Red Cypher's uniform, fighting to breathe as I cried. Eventually, I got a hold of myself, gulping down air as my tears subsided.

When my hands were steady enough to hold it, Cypher helped me gulp a few mouthfuls of water. When he'd filled the glass, I had no idea. I pulled myself up and set the cup down with a dull clunk.

"I'm sorry," I said, dapping the last of the moisture from my eyes. "That wasn't very professional."

"Technically, you're off the clock right now." He assured me. "This is all off the books."

I sniffed. "Doesn't that just work out so well for you and any other wanted criminals who need a consult?"

"I have to remind you once again, you messaged me."

I rolled my eyes and lifted myself from the couch, feeling awkward and exposed. "As though you wouldn't have come anyway. I've been expecting the 'if you say anything it'll be the last thing you do' talk for two weeks."

"I have no intention of hurting you, Velvet," Cypher told me, couch creaking as he stood. "I don't hurt innocent people."

I hesitated and nodded. "So, you'd be willing to help me get in contact with other villains?" I asked.

Cypher barked a laugh. "Are you kidding? They've been seeking me out all day. Every contact point I've got is filled with demands to talk to you. They all want the opportunity to undermine the Super Alliance. If it weren't for me, they'd all be on your doorstep."

My stomach dropped at the thought. "Thank goodness you convinced them otherwise."

"Well, I wanted to give you the option to back out," Red Cypher said.

I frowned in his direction. "What are you talking about? I messaged you."

"Yeah, but I don't think you know what you're getting into."

"Because they're villains?" I asked.

"Exactly." His voice had dropped to an urgent hiss. "Rule number one: never trust a villain."

Anger flared in my chest. "I'm not an idiot. I know not to trust criminals."

"We're talking about criminals with the abilities to manipulate matter, lift trains over their heads and break into your mind. We aren't just your run-of-the-mill bank robbers. These are the people you want to let around children. I need you to think about all the ways this could go wrong and make peace with the fact that it may happen."

I stopped, and I did think about it. Hazard Waste had taken out a city block last year during a battle with Princess Justice. Mistress Medea had shattered a gang boss's pacemaker with her mind, killing him instantly. Road Kill, with his unlimited healing ability, was known to drink and pop pills until he had thrown up his insides.

I buried my face in my hands. "Oh my God, this is a terrible idea."

"I didn't say that," Red Cypher assured me. "I'm merely pointing out it could be a terrible idea."

I lifted my head to glare in his direction. "What's the difference?"

"We set up appropriate preventative measures, try to anticipate any issues which may arise and the most important one, ensure everyone involved is held accountable."

"How are we supposed to do that?" I demanded.

"Do you remember the last time a super villain tried to take over the world, Velvet?" Red Cypher asked, and I blinked in confusion at the sudden shift in topic.

"Er—Professor Nebula?" I recalled. "That was back in the eighties."

Red Cypher leaned against the island right across from me. "After that whole snafu, it occurred to all villains, super or otherwise, if one of us should take over the world or bring about the apocalypse, it wouldn't really benefit the rest of us."

I took a moment to process. "—I suppose not."

"It was just after that the Twilight Syndicate was founded."

"The villain black market?"

"It's quite a bit more," Cypher explained. "Most people think it's just a network passing information and weapons to villains. In reality, it's a way to keep villains in check. The Syndicate makes it hard for anything nefarious to stay secret; if one of us starts to get a bit too ambitious, others will come and put them in their place. Nothing happens without the Syndicate knowing."

I worried my bottom lip between my teeth. "So, they know about me? About all of this?" I asked.

"They aren't thrilled," Cypher acknowledged. "But they have no objection at this time. I think they want to wait and see what happens. Villains or not, there are very few of us who would stand by and allow dying children to come to harm."

"Villains have a code," I mused. "Who'd have thought?"

Cypher chuckled. "It's more of a guideline."

I let out a slow breath. "I understand now why you wanted to warn me. This is way bigger than I could have imagined."

"I'm willing to try." Red Cypher told me. "I enjoyed meeting Charlie. I enjoyed knocking that smug grin off of Black Bullet's stupid face even more. However, I want to make sure you understand what you're getting yourself into. If you get yourself in too deep, you may not be able to get back out."

I thought about Charlie, about the phone call from his mother and the way she described the joy she'd seen in her dying son.

"I want to try," I told him. "I promise to be careful."

Cypher's head dipped in what was most likely a nod. I held out my hand.

"I'm happy to take you and your friends on as clients, Mr. Cypher."

My hand was swallowed by his scarlet-gloved fist. "Call me Red."

Chapter Five

The next day I had five meetings on my schedule before I'd even sat down at my desk.

"A Mr. E just rang for you," Casey said by way of greeting, and the smell of strong coffee accompanied her. The steam hit my face as she set the cup down in front of me.

"Mr. E?" I repeated, eyebrow raised.

"I know, they've all got these really weak aliases." She told me as she scraped a chair across the floor and took a seat across from me. "I decided it was best not to call any of them out on it. "Mr. E is first up after lunch. This morning, we have the parole officer for Emerald Shade and Sharknado."

I choked on my coffee. "Sharknado? I know we need to keep an open mind, but I'm not sure a half-shark man in a hospital is a good idea."

There was a rustle of paper, a notepad being flipped through. "Officer Titas says he got a reduced sentence for good behaviour, and he seemed really excited to meet the kids."

I sighed. "Alright, what else?"

"Mr. H. Watts at ten and Ms. Monique Marquez at eleven. My intel tells me it's Hazard Waste and Mistress Madea. Watts would only do a video conference. Marquez will be in person, but you'll be on your own. I need to take an early lunch."

I rolled my eyes and turned to my computer to do a quick internet search on the two villains. "You're work ethic is exemplary, Casey," I said while the text-to-speech program read out the top results.

"Hey, it's not my fault, I had a manicure booked for today. Georgie didn't take it into account when she gave me the promotion."

I smirked but remained silent while the AI voice read off the stats of each villain.

'Hazard Waste is wanted on three counts of second-degree murder, two counts of manslaughter, five counts of robbery and three of conspiracy to cause harm."

"Hazard Waste is definitely the more *villainous* villain we've dealt with so far." My palms began to sweat. "Are we crazy? Is this crazy?"

Casey made an exasperated noise. "Of course it's crazy. This whole thing is coo-coo bananas, but Georgie can't stop going on about the influx of donations. Apparently, the board has spent most of the night taking calls from shareholders. They're ready to ride this runaway train all the way to the asylum."

"If a kid gets hurt, I'll never forgive myself," I said through clenched teeth.

"Did you talk to Cypher?" Casey asked.

I nodded. "He was in my house last night."

"Sexy," she said.

I huffed. "Oh yeah, breaking and entering really turns me on. Anyway, he said villains have a code, they keep each other in check."

"Do you trust him?" Casey asked.

I chewed the inside of my cheek. "He said rule number one is to never trust a villain."

"Not a bad rule," she agreed. "But you didn't answer my question."

Before I could even open my mouth, Georgie's voice called out from the corridor.

"Velvet! Officer Titus is here."

I closed my browser and told Casey to take notes while I stood to welcome the parole officer.

The morning flew by as I arranged meet and greets, ironed out policies and spouted out so much legal jargon I felt like I'd swallowed a textbook.

The video call with Mr. H Watts was less than productive. He kept his camera off, despite the reassurance that I wouldn't be able to make out his face either way. He insisted on compensation, to which I told him to pound sand.

"We are a non-profit charity," I told him firmly. "You can either donate your time, while abiding by the guidelines I've laid out, or we can end this meeting right now."

"You're a spicy one," he replied in an oily tone which made my skin crawl. "No wonder Cypher likes you."

I ignored the comment. "I'll send over the child's details. It's up to you if you wish to visit or not."

"My time is valuable, Ms. Walker."

"So is mine," I snapped back. "This back and forth is unproductive. If you change your mind, you can contact my assistant for another meeting. Good day."

I ended the call.

"You are a badass," Casey complimented from across the room. "I don't think anyone else would have the balls to stand up to Hazard Waste."

"He's an ass," I muttered. "Though I'm not sure what else I was expecting." I pressed my watch, and a tinny voice let me know it was well after eleven.

"Damn, I'm behind."

"And I'm late," Casey said. She stood, and her footsteps clicked towards the door.

"Is Medea here?" I asked.

"I'll send her in."

The door closed, and I clicked through the tabs on my browser, the AI voice announcing each title, when the room went dark around me.

I chirped out a small squeak of surprise and reached for my cane.

"Good morning, Ms. Walker."

I stiffened. "Mistress Medea, I presume?"

"Umm hmm." Her voice was melodious. It vibrated through the air and up my spine, making me shiver.

"Do you think you could turn the lights back on?" I asked.

"What difference does it make?" She asked. It was impossible to pinpoint her location. Her voice seemed to echo from all around me in the small space.

"I'm not completely blind," I explained, heart fluttering with anxiety. "Not being able to make anything out makes me uneasy.'

"My apologies." The light came back, but they were only the artificial ones. The sunlight streaming through the windows had been blocked out, blinds firmly shut.

I took a breath and reached for the prepared folder. "There are several children who have requested a visit from you. I have—"

"I will see them on one condition." Medea interrupted, her voice now echoing from directly behind me. I jerked my head around but could only make out the dull beige of the office wall.

"I can't offer you compensation," I told her, a headache beginning to form behind my eyes.

"No compensation. In fact, this is beneficial to your non-profit. I will fund it completely from my end."

"What are you talking about?" I asked.

"I want merch." She said.

"Merch?" I repeated dully.

"Merchandise." She repeated, her voice echoing all around. "The Supes have merch, why shouldn't I? I want merch to give out to my adoring fans. T-shirts, plushies, action figures, the works!"

I took a moment to think it over. "I'd need your permission to copyright your likeness. We'd also need to hire an artist to design the items and a third party for manufacturing..."

"Yes, yes," Madea cut me off dismissively. "Send me a list of what is needed, and I will handle everything. I will set up a bank account from which you can draw funds. All money gained will go back to you."

"You mean the Miracle Network?" I clarified.

"If you wish," Madea said. "Though if you wished to keep the profits—"

"No," I told her firmly. "No, I'm not looking to go to jail for embezzlement."

Medea snorted. "Aren't we the law-abiding citizen?"

"Well, I am an attorney." I pointed out.

"Who spent her morning meeting with supervillains?"

I shrugged and turned back to my monitor. "The lesser of two evils, trust me."

"Oo," Medea crooned. A chair scraped across the carpet, and the distinctive creak of the cushion as she took a seat. "Do tell." It was difficult to make out details; it was clear she was keeping herself purposefully indistinct.

"It's not important," I said, weariness overtaking me at the memory. " If you say you'll show up for these kids, then I believe you.

Again, Medea snorted. "Of course. To go back on my word would only enforce pre-conceived notions of all of us."

I smiled softly. "I'll compile all the information you'll need regarding merchandise and contact IT about adding a store to the website."

My computer chimed. "New email from Monique Marquez."

"You may contact me at this email address," Medea explained. "It was set up for me by Red Cypher and is untraceable."

I nodded. "Do you think he might want merchandise as well?" I wondered.

"You would need to ask him," Medea answered, voice flippant, chair squeaking as she stood. "I only care that mine is better and has more rhinestones."

I stood as well, still smiling. "I think I'm going to enjoy working with you, Mistress Medea." I held out my hand.

A beat before she placed her gloved hand in mine and shook. "That says more about you than it does me, Ms. Walker.

Chapter Six

Red Cypher was at my house again. I should've been more annoyed than I was, but he'd brought takeout.

"Curry?" I asked as I dropped my bag in the front entrance.

"From Red Pepper Pot, your favourite." He told me, taking my coat.

"How did you know it was my favourite?" I asked, listening to the jangling of the hangers as he hung the coat in the front closet.

"You ordered it twenty-five times in the last three months."

"You hacked into my delivery app?" I said, stunned.

His scoff was accompanied by the soft click of plates against the countertop. "Nothing so pedestrian, I cloned your phone."

"I didn't hear you say that." I sighed and crossed to the sofa, sinking into the softness gratefully.

The spicy smell of curry wafted through the room. Red crossed the room, settling a plate on my lap.

"Garlic naan and mint sauce," he told me with deliberate pageantry. "You deserve it."

"Why are you doing this?" I asked him. "You can't still think I'm going to turn you over to the Super Alliance."

"Let's not get ahead of ourselves, Ms. Walker." Red cautioned. Settling in beside me, silverware clinking. "One day does not an alliance make."

"I suppose," I agreed, digging into my dinner. "Is that what this is? You're bribing me over to your side with curry?"

Red Cypher was silent for a moment. "You're no villain, Ms. Walker. Nor would I ever wish you to be. I wouldn't wish my life on my worst enemy and certainly not on a well-meaning, pure-hearted woman such as yourself."

I swallowed my mouthful, oddly touched by his words. "How very noble of you."

"As I've said, I'm a villain, not a monster."

"You can call me Velvet, by the way." I insisted.

"Very well." There was an obvious smile in his voice. "That's one of my favourite songs, you know."

I froze, fork halfway to my mouth as a nagging memory began to resurface. "Pardon me?"

"The song by Bobby Vinton." Red went on, casually. "I've had it stuck in my head for weeks because of you." He started to sing, his voice rich and low. "She wore blue velvet..."

I nearly dropped my fork. "M—My mom named me after that song," I told him, heart beating in my throat.

Red paused, and it was infuriating not being able to see his expression, the silence thick with something I couldn't place. After an eternity, he cleared his throat. "It's one of my favourites." He repeated, his voice nonchalant.

I opened my mouth, then closed it. I turned back to the curry quickly cooling on my fork. "I have the vinyl record around here somewhere. My mom would put it on and dance with me when I was little."

"Vintage, I'm liking your mother more and more," I couldn't tell if it was true hesitation in his voice or if I was imagining it. "It's a shame I didn't get to meet her.'

I giggle despite myself. "Probably for the best. A supervillain breaking into my house? She'd come after you with her shotgun."

"You have a shotgun? Red asked, thoughtful.

"My mom did," I repeated. "I sold it after she died."

"Might've been a good idea to keep it around." Red considered. "For protection."

"I've taken plenty of self-defence courses," I told him, stubbornly. "I know how to defend myself."

"You did hold your own against Hazard Waste back at the bar," he agreed. "But it won't always be drunk lowlifes you're dealing with."

"Hazard Waste is hardly a lowlife," I protested around another mouthful. "I've seen his wrap sheet."

Red shrugged. "Eh, say that after you get to know him. I checked his alibi for the night of your mom's murder. I thought he might have come here after you made a fool of him at the bar, but he was caught on security footage blackout drunk on the other side of town."

I took a moment to process. "You believe it was murder, too?"

"You said it was murder," Red pointed out. "I have no reason to doubt you."

"The police don't believe me," I said, a bit too bitterly.

"Tell me why you think she was murdered," Red insisted. "The Police may not want to listen, but I will."

I froze, anxiety paralyzing me in an instant, stealing away the breath from my lungs and causing me to shake uncontrollably.

"Whoa, whoa." Red gripped my shoulder while I struggled to breathe, my chest painfully tight. "Blue, please, breathe for me."

He squeezed my hand in time with his own breathing. The pressure broke through my panic, and I was able to settle ever so slightly.

"I don't—" I exhaled sharply.

"You don't have to," Red assured me. "I shouldn't have brought it up."

I shook my head. Then, "What did you call me?"

I could hear the smile in his voice. "Blue? I didn't—"

I laughed, the sound hurting my chest. "It's fine."

"Are you okay?" he asked.

I swallowed. "Mostly? I guess?"

"Why don't I let you get some rest?" He said rising.

Strange as it was, a part of me didn't want him to leave.

"When will I see you again?"

My phone chimed. *"Contact information shared by Red Cypher."*

"I'll be around," Red promised. "But, if you need to get a hold of me, that's my direct line. Don't go sharing it around."

"Scouts honour," I promised with a giggle.

He took my hand, pressing his lips to the back of it. "Good night, Blue."

I flushed, suddenly desperate to see him. I squinted, fighting through the fog in my vision, as my eyes hunted for the vivid red of his uniform, but it was too dark, lights still off. Red never bothered to turn them on.

"Goodnight," I replied, far too late. He was already gone.

Chapter Seven

"There's a homeless teenager in your office," Casey informed me first thing the next morning.

I groaned. "Why do I feel like I haven't had enough coffee for this yet?"

"Got you covered." A Styrofoam cup was pressed into my hand, the heat of it burning my palm. I stupidly took a sip and immediately scalded the inside of my mouth.

"It's hot," Casey said unhelpfully. "The teenager in question is Ellis Wade aka—"

"Road Kill," I finished with a touch of exasperation. "Should we put a call into the nearest rehab center?"

"He claims he's been clean for a month now," Casey said, though there was more than a little uncertainty in her voice. "He said he's looking for options."

Casey and I strolled into my office, the lights were off, the blinds drawn tight. I frowned more than a little, done with villains and their insistence on darkness. I clicked the switch, the fluorescents burning a white flash into my retinas. A shadowy lump was splayed across my desk, groaning in displeasure.

"Sorry to wake you," I said, striding towards my desk and nearly falling on my face as I tripped on something obstructing my path. My coffee tumbled from my hand, splashing against the carpet and sending a scalding spray over my legs.

"Whoa," Casey called out.

"Sorry!" A hand gripped my arm, pulling me upright. A tingle ran through my fingers and into my arm, down my spine and into my legs. The burning stopped instantly, the stinging now nothing but warm wetness.

"So sorry," Road Kill said again. "Cypher said you were blind, but I'm such a spazz."

"Did you just—heal me?" I asked, astonished.

"Yeah," Road Kill said, rising to help me to my chair. He was shorter than me by at least a head, this and his demeanour reminding me this supervillain was very much still a child. "I have to take on the injury myself. Kinda sucking it out of you into me and then healing it. Takes a bit longer than just healing myself, but you know..."

He trailed off as I sat down, continuing to stand awkwardly at my side until I finally gestured to his vacated seat. He rushed to sit.

Casey cleared her throat. "I'll see about getting that mess cleaned up."

"Thanks, Casey. I'd appreciate another coffee as well. Anything for you, Mister... "

"No, Mister. Just Road Kill," Road Kill said. "I don't drink coffee; the caffeine messes with my powers."

"How bout a donut?" Casey asked. "Gerry brought a bunch in this morning."

"Yeah!" The absolute delight in his voice made my heart clench. "Do you think there's a jelly-filled one?"

"I bet I can track one down, with a bottle of water?"

"Thanks!" Then, with hesitation. "I mean, if it's no trouble."

"I'll be right back."

Once she was gone, I turned my attention fully to Road Kill. A quick sniff of the air told me he probably hadn't had a shower in a good while. Judging by the size of the bag I had tripped over, it was more than likely that it held all of his worldly possessions.

"What can I do for you, Road Kill?" I asked as gently as I could manage.

"I've been hiding out, you see." He began. He was jumpy, the chair squeaking as he twitched from side to side. "I pissed off these gang bangers over on Third Avenue. They got hold of me and started chopping off my toes one at a time. I got away, but it took a while to grow back the toes, you know, and now I've kind of worn out all my welcomes and..."

I held up a hand. "Road Kill, what did you take?"

"Nothing," he insisted.

"I can't help you if you're not honest with me."

"The motherfucker told me it was Oblivion." Road Kill confessed.

I sighed. "Oblivion has been off the market for years."

"They told me it was legit!" He insisted. "They said it would block out my powers."

"You can heal yourself," I said. "Why would you want to block it out?"

"Cause it fucking sucks," he told me. "I heal so fast, I never pass out. I just have to sit and endure, and it's not like I can die. I threw up all my organs and grew them all back."

"Oh god," I said. "Are these gang bangers still looking for you?"

"Ch-yah!" he exclaimed. "That's why I came here. You're a lawyer, right? You can protect me from them, yeah? And you're not allowed to tell the police I'm here, yeah?"

"That's not really how it works." I steepled my fingers as the door opened and Casey strolled back in, her high heels clicking against the carpet.

"One jelly-filled donut and cold water. Gerry said he's just dealing with a clogged toilet and he'll be right up." The last part was directed at me. I'd almost forgotten about the spilled coffee.

Road Kill attacked the donut, the jelly squishing loudly as he bit down. My heart crumbled as I listened to him inhale the food.

"Casey—" I began, but she was already at the door, hinges creaking.

"I'll go grab another one, and I'm pretty sure the sandwiches in the vending machine are still before the expiration date."

"Thank you," I said gratefully. I turned back to Road Kill, now gulping water like he'd just spent a week in the desert. "There are several programs which could help. If you're still a minor—"

He choked, coughing violently. "No, no foster care, no group homes. They treat me like a freak, and the gangs will track me down."

I chewed my lip, uncertain. "Okay, I understand, but if not foster care, then I'm not sure what else I can—"

"Aren't you looking for villains to visit sick kids?" He asked, desperate. "Red Cypher said you had a list comin' out your ass of kids who want to meet villains?"

"Yes," I agreed. "But it's on a volunteer basis. I'm not paying them."

"Oh," Road Kill said, the defeat in his voice was palatable.

I searched desperately for a solution. "We're in the process of setting up a merch store. If you let me copyright your costume, I could set up an account so all proceeds go back to you."

"Don't have a costume," Road Kill said, morosely. "' sides no one wants to buy merch of the guy who threw up his insides on national TV."

I pursed my lips, silently agreeing.

Casey re-entered. "I got a couple of sandwiches and another jelly donut. Velvet, your nine o'clock is here. Should I ask them to wait?"

"Nah, I'm gonna bail." Road Kill's chair was dragged across the carpet. The zipper of his bag was pulled open, and plastic crinkled as he shoved the offered food into its depths. "Thanks for the munchies, much appreciated."

I stood as well. "If you give me time, we can try and work something out."

"S'all good." He shuffled out of the office.

I sat back down, defeated.

"I can push back your nine o'clock." Casey offered.

I shook my head. "No, it's okay, send them in."

Road Kill was in the back of my mind for the rest of the day. I wondered how many others, heroes and villains alike, would be happier without their powers. A quick Google search revealed little on Road Kill or Oblivion. The other villains weren't much help, either.

"Wasn't he the kid who tried to rob a bank and then exploded?" Dr. Nefarious asked. According to Casey, he'd disguised himself as an old woman, complete with the lingering scent of cat urine. "Never met him, and Oblivion hasn't been available for years. Anyway, I'd like you to look at this prototype I'm working on."

I sighed. "I'm legally blind. Can you just summarize it for me?"

"Oh, right," the doctor cleared his throat, embarrassed. "So, these microscopic robots are injected into the bloodstream, and I remotely control them. They could be used to remove tumours which were previously thought to be inoperable."

"That's amazing," I said. "However, to get it approved by the FDA, they'd have to pass through animal and human trials. "

"I've already done several successful human trials." Dr. Nefarious insisted.

"I did not hear you say that," I told him. "Something like this, we would have to go about the legal route. It could take years."

"But this boy you want me to visit, Timmy? He only has a few months."

I nodded, solemnly. "I'm sorry, doctor. There's nothing I can do."

Unsatisfied with my answer, the doctor took his leave, and I took a moment to open the windows and air out the smell of cat.

"We need to get to St. Mary's hospital now!" Casey raced into the office and grabbed me by the arm. I started so violently that I cuffed Casey in the chin. She seemed not to notice as she dragged me towards the door.

"What, why? What's happening?"

"There's currently a standoff at the burn ward between Hazard Waste and the Super Alliance. They've locked down the hospital."

"Oh fuck," I said as she led me as fast as we were able towards the parking lot.

The flashing strobes of press cameras painted the hospital entrance in an erratic burst of white. My cane clicked against the tiles as Casey and I pushed forward, the murmur of voices swelling into a wall of noise.

"Oh shit," Casey said. "They're leading him out in cuffs."

"Shit, shit, shit," I chanted, pushing unseen bodies aside as I fought my way to the front. "I'm Hazard Waste's legal representation!" I called out.

"Fuck you are!" Hazard spat at me, his yellow uniform and vibrant smear. "You set me up. I should have known this was a fucking setup!"

"Your client has a warrant for his arrest," one of the supes told me with utter disdain. "Did you really think we'd let this slide?"

"He was here to visit dying kids," I said, loud enough that every microphone and camera in the vicinity would hear. "He risked everything to fulfil a dying wish, and this is how you treat him? Please tell me you didn't do this in front of the kids."

There was a long pause of hesitation. Cameras flashed in my periphery. "He was resisting arrest."

"You summoned fire in the middle of the burn ward!" Hazard shouted in protest. "You almost hit one of those kids."

The air shifted, and the crowd let out a collective gasp as something dropped out of the sky and landed in the midst of the chaos with a thundercrack of boots against pavement. The crowd erupted in cheers, a chorus of "Black Bullet! Black Bullet! Over here!" drowning out everything else.

"Black Bullet, what's the Super Alliance's official stance on villains fulfilling the wishes of sick children?"

"Black Bullet, it's alleged members of the Super Alliance put civilians in danger during Hazard Waste's arrest. What do you have to say on the matter?"

Black Bullet's arms went up, his black uniform filling my limited sight as he addressed the crowd.

"There's been a terrible misunderstanding," Black Bullet announced with a deliberate, weighted voice. "As of this moment, all medical care centers, hospitals and hospice centers are considered neutral ground. As long as no extreme incidents are reported or safety rules are violated, heroes and villains alike will be able to fulfill their duty to the deserving children of this great city. I will be personally working with Ms. Walker and her office to ensure we can come to a mutually beneficial agreement between our two parties."

The cheer which followed shook the glass doors of the hospital. I knew before the echo faded that Black Bullet's speech would go viral before the six o'clock news. Clipped, replayed and cited in Alliance talking points for weeks to come.

A blur of movement, and I caught the gleam of metal as Black Bullet personally unclasped Hazard Waste's cuffs, slow enough for every lens to catch the action. Then his voice dipped just low enough so only Hazard and the rest of us standing close by could hear.

"Play nice, Waste. The kids are watching, and my mercy only goes so far."

Hazard was jerked toward Black Bullet's side as he wrapped his arm around the villain's shoulder. The cameras went off in another manic burst of flashes. I looked away, a headache slowly forming behind my eyes.

Hazard muttered out a grudging thank you as they posed for the camera, the shutter snapping like applause.

Eventually, Hazard managed to pull himself away, or perhaps Black Bullet had grown tired of sharing the spotlight. He hurried over to where Casey and I waited at the edge of the spectacle.

"I should wring your neck right now," he hissed at me.

"Cameras are still rolling," Casey hissed back. "Go back up to the burn unit and play with the kids."

"Fuck no, I'm getting out of here."

"You run away, the Super Alliance wins," I warned. "You'll just prove them right."

"Weren't you paying attention?" Hazard snapped. "They've already won. One speech, and once again, Black Bullet and his stooges are back on top. He just claimed this whole batshit idea of you as his latest shiny trophy, and I am no one's consolation prize."

I opened my mouth to reply, but he was right. The story was his now, with me and the villains nothing but a footnote.

I groaned, a headache forming behind my eyes.

"Can you just finish the visit?" I begged. "A favour to me? Don't let this all be for nothing."

He breathed for a moment, and though I couldn't see his expression, the weight of his eyes on me was suffocating.

"Fine," he agreed. "You owe me."

"How about a special edition Hazard Waste action figure for the shop?" I suggested. "You can have all the proceeds."

"Forget the proceeds," Hazard relented. "Just make sure every kid in the burn unit gets one."

He stomped away before I could respond, his heavy bootfalls swallowed by the noise of the crowd.

"This really isn't a sustainable business model." I sighed.

"Ms. Walker!" A nearby reporter called out. "A word?"

"Oh, fuck no," Casey muttered. "Let's get out of here."

Casey expertly maneuvered us back through the crowd. Luckily, the reporters still seemed mostly distracted by Black Bullet and the other Alliance member to put up much protest.

Back in the car, Casey's phone screen flashed, her manicured nails clicking rhythmically over the screen.

"Good news! Donations are through the roof. Black Bullet's endorsement has made super villain everywhere a smart investment."

"That was all PR bluster," I said bitterly. "The hammer is going to come down one way or another. The minute we screw up, we'll have every member of the Super Alliance coming for our throats."

"Sooner rather than later," Casey gasped as the taxi pulled up in front of the office. "That didn't take long at all."

"What are you talking about?" I asked.

"MidKnight," Casey answered. "He's waiting outside."

"That's not good," My stomach twisted.

"Murdering piece of shit."

"Allegedly," I said, more of our habit than actual conviction. "The Super Alliance can't have sent him. Black Bullet just declared a truce."

"Unless he's the one they sent to help us come to a *mutually beneficial agreement*," Casey hissed, her tone mocking.

"Are we in danger?" I asked, genuinely frightened.

Casey scoffed. "He's in danger from me. You should call Cypher. I'll go in and get what we need and head to you're place."

However, when Casey opened the door, MidKnight was already there, door in hand, his body blocking out the light.

"Ms. Walker?" MidKnight said, "May I have a word?"

"No, you may not," Casey grunted. She seemed to be fighting for control of the car door. "In fact, you can kindly fuck off."

"I'm afraid I'll have to insist." In one swift movement, MidKnight had pulled Casey out of the back of the cab and taken her place, closing the door behind him. His body filled the small space. His uniform, famously painted with Vantablack, absorbed every scrap of light.

"Take a walk," he said in a voice echoing with power. The driver's side door opened and shut as the driver launched himself from the taxi.

"We have nothing to discuss," I told him, fighting against a tremor in my voice. "Black Bullet and I have come to an understanding."

"Black Bullet had to save face because you backed him into a corner, but there are no kids and cameras to hide behind here. We can speak plainly." MidKnight told me. "You're going to give me all the pseudonyms and contact information you've gathered on the villains and turn over all control of your little pet project to me."

"And then I have every villain in the city out for my blood," I snapped. "No, thank you."

"I would advise you to reconsider." MidKnight insisted. "Consider what would happen should someone, especially a child, get hurt while all these dangerous criminals are trying to play hero. Not only could you be held as an accomplice, but would you be able to live with yourself?"

"You seem to do just fine," I spat, surprising myself. "Considering the Atlanta incident. It wasn't just villains who were killed."

"I'd watch your tongue, Ms. Walker." MidKnight hissed in his echoing baritone. "Someone might just rip it out."

The car door banged open, and MidKnight was yanked from his seat. Casey was at my side in an instant, pulling me out of the taxi. The light of the sun made it impossible to see what was going on after the artificial darkness of the taxi, but I was able to hear several grunts of effort and then a body hitting the pavement.

"What's going on?" I asked Casey.

"I called Cypher," Casey said. "Emerald Shade, Dr. Nefarious and Shockwave came as backup."

"You need to stay the fuck away from her." It was Red's voice, and my entire being relaxed at the sound of it. "Next time you'll have every single villain coming down on your head."

"You are criminals," MidKnight spat back. From the direction of his voice, it seemed as though he was the one on the ground. "You don't get to tell me what to do!"

"Well, we can beat you to bloody pulp if you'd prefer," Emerald Shade suggested.

Nefarious let out a manic laugh. "I do need a new test subject for my present experiment testing the resilience of a Super's pain tolerance."

"You're playing with fire, MidKnight," Red warned. "Step back before you get burned."

MidKnight growled, and I listened to him haul himself up off the ground. Casey turned, tugging me towards the office building, Red following us close enough that I could feel his body heat.

"You watch your back, Velvet Walker," MidKnight called after us.

"Is that a threat?" Casey demanded. "I need to know, so I can include it in my official complaint."

"Then include this," MidKnight snapped, his echoing voice filling the air. "If you continue to consort with villains, it's a promise."

Chapter Eight

The encounter with MidKnight terrified me.

The night found me tucked away in bed while my phone dictated article after article of MidKnight's so-called 'heroism'.

"Suspect found dead after standoff with MidKnight."

"MidKnight accused of misconduct following altercation that left three dead."

"MidKnight's motives called into question following the discovery of a dismembered corpse."

"I'm in way over my head," I told Casey the next morning when she showed up at my front door. I'd been ready to call in sick when she'd shown up.

She whisked her way into my house, the smell of fresh coffee and croissants wafting through the room. She took my phone out of my hand and forced me onto the couch; a warm cup was placed in my hand.

"Drink," she said. Her accent is thick and prominent. "Breathe."

I obeyed, the rich coffee breaking through the anxious haze in my mind.

"MidKnight is a raging bag of dicks," She confirmed. "But the Supes have him on a short leash. 'sides, I passed two villains incognito and one very obvious camera disguised as a potted plant on my way here. Trust me, *liebchen*, he's not getting near you."

I wiped my face on the corner of the duvet. "Two villains?"

"Dr. Nefarious, in his ridiculous old woman get up and Hazard Waste in a trench coat with a newspaper sitting at the bus stop. They think they are so sneaky."

I laughed despite myself. "I guess I shouldn't be surprised. They need to make sure I'm not going to go turncoat on them."

"Meh," Casey shrugged. "At this point, there's little harm you could do with the information you have. I think they like you, or at least, like the chaos you're helping to create. But Velvet,"

Casey paused and put a hand on my knee. "You don't have to continue. We can stop this right now, no hard feelings."

I took a breath, inhaling the soothing scent of coffee. "How many requests are we up to?"

"For villain visits?" Casey's fingers tapped her phone screen. "Three hundred and thirty-six. We've got families from states over getting in contact."

I sighed. "Then we've got work to do."

With my safety in question, Georgie gave us her blessing to work from home indefinitely. The first order of business was to find a secure way to communicate with clients (calling them villains left a bad taste in my mouth).

Red Cypher, of course, was instrumental in creating a segregated Discord with a revolving IP that allowed us to send messages and have meetings which couldn't be traced.

Over the next few weeks, we managed to make the process of pairing clients with children practically seamless, though the paperwork was never-ending.

Every news outlet imaginable had seized onto the story, running updates nonstop of children overjoyed at the presence of super villains in their hospital rooms.

"Ten-year-old Charlie Glynn was the first child the Miracle Network was able to pair with a super villain." According to the screen description, Charlie was showing off the modification Red Cypher had made to his laptop.

"I know some people are saying they're bad people," Charlie told the camera. "But, even if that's true, Red Cypher took a big risk coming to see me, and I'll forever be grateful."

"Tough kid," Casey commented, keyboard clicking as we filled out yet another copyright form.

I blinked away tears. "Tough, smart. It's not fair."

My phone rang, Casey answered. After my number had been leaked a few weeks back, she'd taken particular glee in dressing down any angry callers.

"Velvet Walker's phone." A pause. "Really? That's very exciting. Could you have your executive send over confirmation? Tuesday? Yes, I can clear her schedule. Excellent." The call ended.

"Good news," Casey said. "You're going to be a guest on *Masks Off*."

I stood up, spilling papers and my tablet to the floor. "Absolutely not."

"What?" Why not?" Casey demanded.

"I haven't left my house in almost a month, and now you want me to go on a national talk show?"

"Absolutely! You need to get out of the house!"

"It's too dangerous. Also, it'll be completely biased in the super's favour. The whole network is run by Titan Global."

Casey made a non-committal noise. "They're calling you the Villain Wrangler, you know and Blind Justice. That one is my favourite."

I crossed my arms but said nothing.

"You're becoming a sensation in your own right. You're the face of the villain revolution." Casey went on. "You need to be their voice as well."

I took a breath. "Am I really the best person for it?"

"You're the only person for it," Casey insisted. "You decided the moment you tracked down Cypher at *The Silent Duke*."

I frowned, wondering exactly when I'd mentioned the name of the bar to Casey, when my phone rang again.

"Velvet Walker's phone." There was a long, heavy pause. "I see. I'll let her know—yes. Yes, she'll definitely be there. My condolences."

My heart dropped as I listened to the line disconnect. "What happened?"

Casey sighed, "Charlie died this morning."

Chapter Nine

The funeral became national news. The media was held back by a police tape and prayers as we filed into the church. Charlie's parents found me immediately, pulling me in for grateful hugs.

"We owe you so much." Charlie's mother told me through tears. "Charlie died talking about the upgrades Red Cypher had been sending him. He was smiling."

My throat closed, my tongue going numb in my mouth. Thankfully, Casey noticed and took over, thanking the parents and leading me away to a quiet corner to regroup.

"Here," a voice said, pressing a cool plastic bottle into my hand.

"Nice of you to show up, Cypher." Casey snarked.

"Red," I breathed, overwhelmed with gratitude at his presents. From what I could tell, he was in disguise, no hint of his customary red uniform.

"Drink," he urged. "It's going to be a long day."

"Stay with me?" I begged.

He took my hand, lacing his fingers through mine. "For as long as you want me."

It was odd how relieved I felt with Red next to me as we took our seats.

"Black Bullet is here," Casey noted.

"Fuck him," I muttered. "Did any other clients make it?"

Red hummed in confirmation. "Medea and Hazard are here incognito. I see Emerald Shade and Shockwave. Dr. Nefarious and Sharknado said they would try and make it. The whole fucking Super Alliance is here, taking up the front row like their shit doesn't stink. No, MidKnight, guess they didn't want to risk an incident."

I refused to think about the implications, forcing myself to relax for the first time in what felt like weeks, the echoing murmurs of the crowd washing over me.

"Velvet doesn't want to do the *Masks Off* interview," Casey stated, the paper program crinkling in her hand as she flipped through the pages.

I nearly growled, heart rate rising. "Casey." I snapped.

"What?" I could hear the pout in her voice.

I glared at her. "We're not talking about this right now."

"Wouldn't hurt to get Cypher to weigh in," Casey said.

"It's Velvet's choice," Red stated firmly. "She'll do what she believes is right."

The pinching tightness in my chest released ever so slightly. "Thank you," I whispered.

He squeezed my hand.

Casey gave an irritated hum. "The audacity."

I rolled my eyes. "Behave yourself, we're at a funeral."

"Me?" She asked, eyes so wide the top of her head looked completely white. "I'm innocent, I've never done a bad thing in my life."

"Casey—"

"I was born yesterday."

Red raised his hand and, to my horror, whacked Casey across the top of her head.

"Rude!" she huffed.

"Red!" I snapped.

"Sorry," he murmured. "Got carried away."

Music began to play. "Both of you stop it!" I demanded as the service began.

It was difficult not to be reminded of my mother's funeral and the events surrounding her death while the service progressed. It became hard to focus, my mind drifting back to that night, the sounds and smells. The sour stink of vomit seemed permanently fixed in my nose. I swallowed hard, sweat beading on my forehead. I leaned forward, feeling sick.

"Velvet?" Casey placed a hand on my back. The pews around us creaked and banged as people rose.

"Sorry," I said to no one in particular.

"There's a car waiting to take us to the graveyard," Casey informed me. "Unless you're not feeling up to it."

"No," I stood, only a tad unsteady. "No, I'm fine."

"Black Bullet is coming over here," Red informed me.

"Fuck," I said, trapped by the crowd. It was nearly impossible to differentiate between people in the mass of roiling black.

"Ms. Walker," Black Bullet called, his voice carrying easily over the murmuring congregation. "A word."

"We've got a car waiting." Casey was suddenly in front of me, her black pantsuit prominent in my limited vision, though just as quickly as she had appeared, she was pushed away, Black Bullet's hand enclosing around my arm.

My blood ran cold, and Red tensed at my side.

"I won't be a moment."

I swallowed. The crowd had slowed around us, the hot pinpricks of their gazes making my chest tight. "Let go of me and we can talk."

His hand dropped from my arm as though burned. "I've been made aware you are scheduled for an interview on *Masks Off*."

"Yes," I replied.

"I would greatly discourage it."

"Why?" Casey hissed. "Are you going to send MidKnight after us again?"

Black Bullet ignored her. "Putting yourself center stage like that only hurts your reputation and gives people the wrong idea."

"Titan Global is the one who authorized it," I pointed out. "It's their network."

"It was authorized against my wishes." Black Bullet said, bitterly. "They seem to have the wrong idea about how your entire operation should be handled."

I bristled. "The only thing you're worried about is your reputation. Heaven forbid you and your team of so-called heroes look bad in the eyes of the public."

"How is MidKnight by the way?" Casey asked casually. "Any more skeletons fall out of his closet on the way back to headquarters?"

Black Bullet was silent for a long moment. I was ready to push past him when he finally spoke.

"I looked up Samuel Hall." He told me.

"Good for you," I snapped back.

"I realize I failed that poor boy."

"Wow, self-reflection, what an excellent display of growth. Now, if you'll excuse us, we have a car waiting." I pulled on Red's arm; he seemed momentarily frozen in place, but quickly thawed and hurried after Casey and me.

"Who's Samuel Hall?" Casey asked once we'd made it to the car. Beside me, Red kept a death grip on my hand, his whole body oddly tense.

I swallowed. "A kid I worked with a few years back. I don't really want to get into it right now."

"Alright," Casey agreed, and Red put a comforting arm around my shoulders.

Silence fell over us. I listened to the sounds of traffic outside, considering.

"Casey,"

"Yeah?"

"Call *Masks Off*, tell them I'll do the interview."

Chapter Ten

"Welcome back to *Masks Off*, your news source for all things super. I'm Stacy Shepherd, and if you're just joining us, today our special guest is attorney Velvet Walker, aka The Villain Wrangler, aka Blind Justice. Velvet, thank you so much for being here today."

The studio lights were too bright for me to even begin to make anything out. Instead, I sat back in the uncomfortable armchair and tried my best to face Stacy.

"Thanks for having me." I tried to sound confident, but it came out as a squeak.

"Your work for the Miracle Network has become a very decisive topic in the media as of late. Would you like to fill in our viewers who may have been living under a rock these last few weeks?"

The studio audience laughed, and I waited for the last of it to subside before launching into the story of Charlie's wish to meet Red Cypher and tracking him down.

"The courage it must have taken to confront a supervillain," Stacy commented after I described mine and Red's first meeting.

"In retrospect, the word I would use is stupid." Again, the audience laughed. I went on. "Red Cypher showed me and Charlie more decency than I could have imagined from someone society had labelled a 'villain'. Our partnership had led to giving an entire community of marginalized individuals a second chance."

"People have been quick to point out these are criminals we are talking about," Stacy said.

I nodded, "That's exactly why we've partnered with the penal systems and work placement programs. As of today, we've had three convicts take a combined three months off their sentences by visiting sick kids in the hospitals."

"And the ones who are not incarcerated?" Stacy asked.

"I'm afraid that falls under client confidentiality," I told her with a smile.

"But you did acknowledge your partnership with Red Cypher."

I found myself blushing despite myself. "I—er—more a mutual beneficial relationship."

I, of course, couldn't see his face, but there was a certain knowing in Stacy's tone when she spoke. "Ah, yes, very beneficial, I can gather.

"Tell me, Velvet, has your work with the supervillain been influenced in any way by the death of your mother?"

I froze, blood turning to ice in my veins. "We didn't discuss—"

Stacy ploughed on, unconcerned. "An apparent suicide on the same day you first encountered Red Cypher, though according to the police report, you maintained it was murder, what made you reach that conclusion?"

"Did Black Bullet feed you that information?" I shot back, voice oddly detached, heart pounding a painful rhythm against my chest.

"It's public record," Stacy spluttered, but it was clear to me Black Bullet must have gotten into her ear.

"Black Bullet pulled me aside at Charlie Glynn's funeral and told me not to do this interview," I said. "We hadn't even put him in the ground yet, and the leader of the Super Alliance was more occupied with what I might say about him."

Stacy Shepherd laughed uncomfortably. "Maybe it's a good time to head to commercial..."

"Two years ago, I asked Black Bullet to come visit a seven-year-old with an inoperable brain tumour, named Samuel Hall. He cancelled three times, and when he finally showed up, he took one blurry selfie and threw a signed photograph at the poor kid. All without saying one word to any of us. It wasn't even the kid's phone; it was mine." I took a breath and stared in the direction of where I hoped the camera would be. "I work with supervillains because superheroes have let me down time and time again. My mother was murdered; a dying little boy was let down by his greatest hero. It's as simple as that. Thank you for having me."

I pulled the microphone from my shirt and picked up my cane, picking my way carefully backstage. It was unfortunate that being blind made it very hard to storm off properly, but I did my best.

Once away from the blinding lights, I leaned against the nearest wall and fought back tears of humiliation. "That was stupid," I murmured brokenly, under my breath.

"Ms. Walker?" a voice said at my elbow. "Your assistant is waiting for you in the green room. Can I take you there?"

I nodded, grateful and allowed myself to be taken by the arm and led through the maze-like studio. I could only imagine Casey's reaction to the hijacking of the disastrous interview.

We'd been walking for quite a while, my whole body felt heavy, and I longed to sit down and rest.

"How much farther?" I asked. A door was opened, and I was urged into an oddly dark room.

"Nice to see you again, Velvet."

My whole body tensed, reacting to the voice before my brain had even placed it.

"MidKnight."

A sharp poke in my neck, and something cool and numbing was injected into my veins. I slumped forward, blacking out before I could hit the floor.

Chapter Eleven

I blinked and found myself cloistered in a dark room, tied to a chair. It was easy not to panic with my brain still full of fog, though with every heartbeat, my senses grew clearer and my chest grew tighter.

"Good, you're awake," a voice spoke, the sound seemed to come from all around me. "We can get started."

A wad of material was pulled from my mouth, and I choked from the unexpected sensation. I bent over as far as I could, coughing violently into my lap. A glass was pressed to my lips, but I jerked away, the move causing the glass to tumble to the ground and shatter.

"That's a poor way to show appreciation for our hospitality."

"Fuck you!" I shouted, fighting for air.

A fist caught me just under my ribcage, and my vision went white with pain. The little air that had been in my lungs left with a painful woosh.

Ears ringing, my breathing was a harsh wheezing as I fought to inflate my lungs.

"Let's jump straight to the point, shall we?" It was MidKnight's voice, the heat of his body mere inches from me. "You're going to give me all the information you have on all the supervillains you've allied yourself with, and then I'm going to kill you."

Barely able to breathe, I lifted my head in the direction of MidKnight's voice. "Not much of a negotiation," I said, mind fuzzy.

"Oh, your death is non-negotiable," he told me with a sickening amount of glee. "What I can assure you is that if you cooperate, I'll make sure it's quick and mostly painless. However," a hand fisted in my hair, jerking my head painfully up, until I could feel MidKnight's hot, vile breath on my face. "If you decide to be difficult, then I have no problem taking my time."

I spat in his face, which probably wasn't the smartest thing I could have done. I couldn't quite find it in myself to regret it, even as he backhanded me across the face.

Despite my show of defiance, I was very much starting to panic. Smothered by the darkness, at the mercy of a sociopath masquerading as a hero, I privately wondered why I hadn't seen this coming. Of course, this was where working with supervillains was going to get me: tortured, murdered, body dumped in a shallow grave somewhere, never to be seen again.

"Now, I want names, aliases, contact information and everything you have on the drug Oblivion."

"Why the hell would I know anything about Oblivion?" I gasped, genuinely confused.

"Oh, don't play me," MidKnight spat. "You're the only person alive who knows, and Black Bullet wants that formula."

"I have no fucking idea what you're talking about." I wheezed, heart banging in my chest. MidKnight slapped me with so much force that my chair toppled backwards. My head slammed against the cement floor. He pulled it back upright, my head jerking forward as I fought to stay conscious.

"Good," MidKnight said, delighted. "I was hoping to have a bit of fun."

He circled me, crouching down to where my hands were tied behind my back and took the index finger of my left hand in his. In one swift motion, he snapped the bone.

My scream bounced off the walls in a macabre orchestra.

"Let's start with something easy," He began. "Where do you keep your client contact list?"

I swallowed, chest heaving as my mind fought through the pain. "Up your ass," I spat.

My pinky finger was snapped in two. I shrieked until my throat was raw, tears streaming down my face.

"Where did your mother keep her research files?" MidKnight demanded, but I was in too much shock to process the question. He shook the chair, the jarring motion sending renewed spikes of pain shooting through my chest.

"We can do this all—"

There was a deafening cracking noise, and I braced myself, but my remaining fingers miraculously remained intact. Through my ringing ears, I was able to make out a dull thud and a grunt of pain.

"How the hell did you find me!" MidKnight shouted. I heard a fist striking flesh and then a bang as something heavy collapsed to the floor.

Gentle gloved hands moved to untie me. "The fact that he assumed I wouldn't be tracking your every move is a little insulting. Still, MidKnight has never been known for his intelligence. Who else would grab someone right after they'd been on national TV?"

"Red!" I gasped, relieved tears overflowing down my cheeks. He did away with the ropes and pulled me into his arms, squeezing me tight.

"I'm sorry it took me so long. He had a way to scramble the signal. I managed to get a ping at this location when he moved you from the car to the warehouse."

I burrowed into him, my uninjured hand sliding against his armour, the surface cool on my skin. Then a moment later, I was tumbling backward as Red was wrenched away from me, his body crashing to the floor.

"Worthless piece of shit," MidKnight rasped, his words heavy and forced. "I'm going to feed you your own heart."

"No thanks," Red replied, light rippled over my vision, the smell of ozone filling my nose as electricity cracked across the room, making my hair stand on end. A body crashed to the floor.

"Medea is always telling me to double-tap," Red groaned, body shifting and creaking in a way that sounded painful. "I should've listened."

"Is—is he dead?" I asked, too scared to move.

There was a grunt of effort, the sound of something heavy being dragged or rolled.

"He's breathing," Red confirmed. He left the fallen superhero and gathered me up in his arms. "That might change once everyone finds out about this."

"No one will believe us."

"They'll believe the camera footage," he said. "I planted one on the button of your blouse."

I cradled my injured hand gingerly, while the other felt the smooth surface of each button.

"Is that how you found me?" We'd entered a larger space, my voice echoed slightly, and I could just make out the distant sound of traffic.

"No, I had Nefarious whip up some of his nanobots with trackers. I slipped them into your curry. They entered your bloodstream and embedded into your tissues."

He said it very matter-of-factly, with no hint of remorse. There was a beep, a car honked, and the doors unlocked. I was placed into the passenger seat the seatbelt fastened around me.

"I feel like I should be angry?" I said after he'd taken the driver's seat.

He revved the engine and started to drive. "Are you?" he asked.

"No," I told him.

"Good," he said, then, "Are you in pain?"

The throbbing came back to me then, now that some of the adrenaline had worn off. My hand felt two sizes too big, the broken digits throbbing.

"He broke two of my fingers and I think a couple of ribs," I said, forcing out the words between breaths. "I definitely have a concussion."

"Hospital then," he said.

"I don't want you to have to go," I begged, terrified at the thought.

"Never said I was," Red assured me. "If memory serves, hospitals are still neutral ground."

Unsurprisingly, Red was recognized immediately. Though not at all in the way I'd expected.

"Mr. Cypher? What are you doing in the Emergency Room, the pediatric—Oh my god! Get me a bed!"

I was set down on the hardest mattress I'd ever felt, while a dozen people blurred around me, connecting me to beeping machines and sticking me with needles. Red's gloved hand stayed firmly in mine. I kept my focus on the scarlet of his uniform while the doctors and nurses asked me questions.

"What's your name?"

"Velvet Walker."

"Do you know where you are right now, Velvet?"

"The hospital."

"Do you remember what happened?"

"Yes, but it's a long story."

"Are you experiencing dizziness? Nausea? Blurred vision?

"Yes."

"Velvet, can you look right here?" A light flashed in my eyes, and I jerked away.

"She's blind," Red told them.

"Partially blind," I snapped back. "Pinhole blindness caused by dry macular degeneration. Don't answer for me."

"I'm terribly sorry," Red murmured, his voice amused, which irritated me even more. I closed my eyes and lay back against my pillow, utterly exhausted.

"We'll take you up for a CT scan. It looks like you have a concussion. Are you injured anywhere else?"

"My ribs," I said, pulling at my blouse. "My hand too."

My shirt was pushed up, and I heard the doctor curse under his breath.

"Call the OR, tell them we've got a possible collapsed lung."

"Surgery?" Red exclaimed. "Is that really necessary?"

"Yes, and we need to go now." The bed jerked and began rolling forward.

"Red," I gasped, finding it harder and harder to breathe. My grip on his hand tightened, jerking my body back as he ran to keep up.

"I'll be here when you get out, Velvet." He promised, "It's going to be alright."

My fingers went to my blouse buttons. I focused hard, my brain feeling like it was splitting apart as I fingered each button and immediately ripped out the one not made of polymer plastic. I pressed it into Red's hand.

"Fuck them up for me," I told him as his fingers slipped away, the bed banged, and doors swung violently on their hinges as I was rushed up into surgery.

Chapter Twelve

As promised, Red was there when I woke up, his hand clasped tightly in mine.

"Red," I breathed. My chest felt hollow, the air echoing in its vastness. My other hand was bound in a cast, along with my chest. Nearby, a machine beeped quietly.

"Bout time you woke up," another voice said from the other side of the bed. I squinted, trying to make out the figure.

"Casey is here," Red told me. "Along with Hazard Waste and Dr. Nefarious."

"Wha—" the word was cut off by a cough. My mouth felt like the Sahara Desert. A cup was pressed to my lips, and I gulped down the water like I'd never get another drop.

"They insisted," Red explained. "After everything, I felt better with the extra muscle around."

Casey snorted. "Muscle? From that pipsqueak?"

I assumed she meant Dr. Nefarious as he began to splutter in indignation. "You'll be happy I came when she walks out of here in half the time it would take those law-abiding doctors to cure her."

Alarmingly, the not-so-good doctor appeared to be fiddling with the machines beside the bed. The needle in my arm tugged painfully, while the machines beeped in disapproval.

"Hey," I protested, the words like cotton in my mouth. "Knock that off."

"Told you she wouldn't like it," Casey commented, over the tapping of a keyboard.

Dr. Nefarious snorted dismissively. "Do not fear, Velvet. This method has gone through several rounds of human testing."

"I didn't hear that," I groaned.

"In the meantime, you can tell us exactly what happened between you and MidKnight." Hazard Waste all but demanded. Something, most likely his fist, clanged against the metal bedframe.

"I told you no interrogations," Red snapped. "You saw the video."

"Videos can be doctored," Hazard insisted. "I need to look into someone's eyes to know if they're lying."

"Oh, fuck off," I told the room in general. Then the true meaning of Red's words hit me like a lightning bolt.

"The video," I said, squeezing his hand. "Did you—"

"Currently trending worldwide," Casey supplied happily. "Original video currently at seven hundred thousand views, two hundred thousand shares. The supes are scrambling to do damage control. At first, they tried to say the video was a fake, but then word got out that MidKnight had been removed from the Alliance. People are furious, they're calling for an arrest, it's a madhouse." She sounded positively delighted

I lay back, the hospital-issue pillow crinkling under my head. "Good," I murmured, eyes heavy.

"Rest, Velvet." Red urged. "We can deal with everything else later."

It was possibly the best advice I'd ever been given. I gladly closed my eyes and went back to sleep.

I stumbled my way back into the waking world hours later, opening my eyes to pitch darkness and Casey's hushed voice.

"—still recovering. Also, I'm insisting upon extra security and a list of questions agreed upon in advance. No deviations, understood?"

"Mm...Casey?" I rasped. My mouth was drier than it had ever been in my entire life. I struggled to unstick my tongue from my gums.

"I've got to go." A clink, as something solid, probably a cellphone, was set on a table, and a squeak as Casey moved to my side. "Hey, how are you feeling?"

"—Time is it?"

"Ten thirty-four." She said, "Are you thirsty? Hungry?"

"Yes," I replied, my stomach roaring its displeasure. A cup of water was placed at my lips. I reached up to grasp it, downing the water in three large gulps. I smacked my chapped lips. "More, please. Where's Red?"

"I'm not sure." The sound of pouring water cut off in favour of a drawer being opened. "Red?" Casey said to the room at large. "Red Cypher?"

I laughed, "What the fuck are you doing?"

"Looking for Cypher."

"Fuck you."

She laughed. "No thanks, I'm not my type. I think he must be getting you something to eat. The only thing the nurses had was a tiny packet of crackers, and Nefarious managed to scarf those when we weren't looking."

"Pretty on brand for a villain," I acknowledged. "Did he and Hazard get bored and take off?"

"Uncertain," Casey admitted. "Nefarious said he had some things to check in on. I'm pretty sure Hazard is running surveillance from outside. There's a bunch of press out there."

"What are they saying?" I asked.

"Oh, lots of things," Casey said. "People are split on whether MidKnight was just acting in the best interest of the Super Alliance, or if he was way out of line and should face jail time."

"It was in the best interest of the Super Alliance to punch my face in?" I asked bitterly.

"According to Black Bullet, he was working on his own. Here, he held a press conference."

She pulled up the video on her phone and passed it to me. I didn't bother squinting at the screen and just listened as Black Bullet addressed the press.

"To be clear, we are not giving villains amnesty from their crimes." Black Bullet insisted, his voice echoing through the microphone. "We have partnered with the Miracle Network to ensure every child is given the hope and care they deserve, and if that hope comes from a visit with a villain, we want to ensure they aren't caught in the crossfire of our conflicts."

"But isn't that the same as legitimizing villains? Aren't you worried you're giving them a platform to undermine the Super Alliance?" A reporter questioned.

"We are not legitimizing anyone. We are merely doing what is in the best interest of the children. If anyone dares step outside the rules we've set in place, they'll answer to me personally. That includes MidKnight and his baseless attack on Velvet Walker. He will be held accountable for his actions."

The was a ripple of approving murmurs. A few flashbulbs popped, and another reporter jumped in, voice sharp.

"Black Bullet, in the video of the attack. MidKnight accuses you of trying to obtain the formula for Oblivion. Oblivion hasn't been seen in the last few years. Why would you be interested in the formula?"

Black Bullet cleared his throat. "It's true I have been investigating the source of Oblivion. It is a dangerous drug that nearly destroyed this city when it was on the streets. Its ability to strip powers from powered individuals destabilized lives, crippled defences and left us vulnerable. The Super Alliance worked tirelessly to wipe it out, and intelligence tells us the source may still be out there, and if Oblivion does resurface, in the wrong hands, entire teams of superheroes could be neutralized in seconds. It is my goal to prevent that from happening at all costs."

"What about the rumours you intend to weaponize Oblivion yourself to use against villains?"

"Heroes do not win by tearing others down." Black Bullet told the crowd, his tone full of magnitude and bluster. "We win by standing tall and supporting each other. Together, we will continue to protect this great city. Thank you."

"He didn't actually answer that last question," I noted as I handed Casey her phone back.

"A true politician," Casey agreed. "Anyway, don't worry about him or anything else right now. I've got it covered."

"I worry slightly." Red's voice was accompanied by the rich smell of garlic and curry.

"Oh my god," I said, inhaling. "I love you."

The room went silent, and my face burned at the realization of what I said.

"I mean, not that—because of the curry—urg."

Red chuckled, and the sound sent a tingle of pleasure through my aching body. "It's okay, Blue. Let me help you sit up."

When I was settled, happily gulping spicy mouthfuls, Casey took the opportunity to slip out.

"I'll be back in the morning. There are a few fires I need to either put out or fan the flames. I'll decide when I get there."

I squeaked out a goodbye around a mouthful of naan. Once she was gone, Red and I sat in companionable silence while I finished my meal. After the containers had been disposed of, he took my hand again. Something about his grip on my fingers made me take pause.

"What is it?" I asked.

"I have a question," Red admitted. "But I don't want to upset you unnecessarily."

My blood ran cold, while my mind attempted to sort through the possibilities. It was impossible to do while my brain was marinating in pain meds.

Red continued, despite my silence. "Back in the ER, before they wheeled you away, you touched each button on your blouse and managed to pick out the camera on the first try. I went out of my way to make sure it was indistinguishable from the others, and you picked it out by touch."

I took a breath, heart racing. "That's not really a question."

"Are we using Jeopardy rules?" he asked, a smile in his voice.

There were a million logical reasons why I should lie. Chiefly among them was Red, who had told me to never trust a villain. However, logic and self-preservation had gone out the window the moment MidKnight had abducted me.

"I can tell the chemical properties of anything I touch," I admitted. "My mom could do it too, but she was way stronger. She could replicate things to a degree, which really came in handy when dealing drugs."

"That's impressive," Red said.

"Not really," I said. "I can only identify things I've encountered before. I just picked the button that wasn't the same as the others."

Red was silent. I listened to his breathing, feeling strangely at peace, despite myself.

"Thank you for being honest with me," Red said, eventually. "Is this ability part of the reason you think your mother was murdered?"

"Yes," I whispered. "When I found her, my mom was covered in DNA that wasn't hers. The police dismissed it because of her past, but I know there was someone else there that night."

"If you want to track down her killer, I'll help you anyway I can," Red promised.

I shook my head. "What I want is to expose every single member of the Super Alliance. Hang their dirty laundry out for everyone to see."

"Are you sure?" Red asked, "Velvet, you nearly died."

"So what?" I demanded. "If they came for me once, there's no reason to think they won't do it again. I'm done hiding."

"You are incredible," Red told me. "And as soon as I know that's not just the pain medication talking, we'll get started."

Chapter Thirteen

The hospital was forced to release me two days later, after my seemingly miraculous recovery. Bones had knit themselves together, blood replenished, punctured lung completely mended.

"I'm going to go ahead and chalk this up to a miraculous recovery and ignore any modifications a certain villain may have made to your IV." The doctor told me as he unwrapped my fingers, now back in one piece.

"We need to make a stop at pediatrics," I told Red as he wheeled me down to the elevator in the completely unnecessary wheelchair the nurses had insisted upon.

"As you wish," Red replied, the elevator dinging and the wheelchair bumping as I was pushed inside. "Let's make it quick, though. I'd like to get you home."

"I'm fine," I insisted. "Nefarious has convinced me."

"Convinced you?" Red asked. Before I could reply, the elevator dinged again, opening onto the children's ward.

"Velvet!" Someone called. I squinted and managed to make out a bleached blond blob of hair.

"Hatty!" I replied, accepting her brief embrace.

"It's good to see you up and around," Hatty exclaimed. "Is Mr. Cypher taking good care of you?"

"Whether I like it or not," I laughed.

"I saw your interview on *Masks Off*." Hatty gushed. "Good for you, making them face their demons. I remembered that boy, Sam, wasn't it? His father was so angry, I took him to the family room to cool off."

"Oh," I said, surprised. "I didn't realize you were there that day."

"Oh yes," Hatty said. "It was an emotionally charged day for all of us. I told Aiden, the father, I mean, his name was Aiden Hall, he should make an official complaint, but that suggestion didn't go over too well. I wonder how he's doing."

"Hatty, is Timmy still here?" I said, interrupting her musings.

"Hm? Timmy?" Hatty said, her voice suddenly grave. "He's in and out of consciousness. It won't be long now."

I frowned, uncertain. "What room?"

"Thirty fourteen."

"Okay," I stood from the chair and turned to Red. "Come on."

"Velvet what—?" Hatty asked, but I held a hand up.

"We weren't here," I told her with a wink. "You didn't see anything."

"Okay—" Her voice was hesitant, but she didn't stop us as Red led me to the room, the air full of beeping machines and pumping vents.

"Oh, Ms. Walker." Timmy's mom said before we'd even crossed the threshold. "It's so good to see you. How are you doing?"

"I'm fine," I said, taking the seat Red led me to. "How are you?"

"Taking everything day by day," she admitted. "Timmy's dad is having a hard time. He left to clear his head."

I took a breath, steadying myself. "What if I had another option for Timmy?" I blurted.

"Pardon me?"

Another breath. "One of my clients has an unlicensed medical procedure he thinks may help Timmy."

"Unlicensed?" Timmy's mom repeated, skeptical.

"It's a completely new technique developed by my client. You need to understand this is nowhere near sanctioned by any medical board, anywhere. You'd need to relocate Timmy to another facility, and no one can know."

"It's Dr. Nefarious, isn't it?" She guessed. "He said something about reprogramming tiny robots during his visit. He thinks he could really help Timmy."

"He helped me," I told her. "Granted, I didn't have a tumour pressing on my brain."

"How soon could he do it?" She asked.

"Tomorrow," Red spoke from behind me. "This is the address. He'll be waiting, ready for whenever you're able to get him discharged."

A shadow passed by my line of sight as Red handed something to Timmy's mom.

"I can't promise this will work," I told her. "If it doesn't—"

"It's not like we have a lot of options." Timmy's mom sniffed. The machines beeped. "Thank you, Ms. Walker."

I nodded and allowed Red to lead me from the room, down out of the hospital to the waiting car.

I fell asleep almost immediately. The trek through the hospital was enough to completely exhaust me. It wasn't until I was being lifted from the passenger's seat by strong, secure arms that I finally roused.

"What changed your mind?" Red asked as he carried me into the house.

"MidKnight's fist in my gut," I replied, resting my head against his chest, the sound of his heartbeat soothing. "Really made me rethink the difference between the heroes and villains."

"Ah, yes," Red replied, ascending the staircase, the floor creaking underfoot. "Because villains will look you in the eye while they kill you, while a hero will always wait till you're not looking, stab you in the back and convince everyone it was your fault."

It was obviously supposed to be a joke, but there was such a bitter undertone that I couldn't laugh. I reached up and cupped his cheek, turning his face so he would look at me.

"I think there's quite a bit more to it," I told him.

"Yes?" he said, laying me down on my bed, the familiar comforter soft and inviting. "What else?"

He tried to rise, but I held tight, pulling him down with me.

"Velvet—" he began, but I pulled his face to mine and stole the words right out of his mouth. The kiss was brief, his warm lips pressing against mine for only a moment before retreating. I could feel his gaze on me, his grip on my arms loosening.

"Don't," I told him.

"Velvet," he said again. "You don't want this."

"I thought I told you not to answer for me," I snapped, wrapping my arms around his neck and pulling him toward me. This time, he gave in, moulding his body to mine, kissing me with a ferocity I recognized from every interaction we'd had. From the first moment confronting him in that seedy little bar, to the way he'd bonded himself to me, without either of us realizing.

He pulled away again, and I growled in frustration. "Stop doing that. I want this, just accept it."

"You don't even know who I am."

"Yes, I do," I said with conviction. "I don't need to see your face to know who you are."

"I'm a villain," he said, his voice sounding pained, as though just barely on the edge of control.

"I'm very aware, Red," I told him.

"I'm older than you," He went on.

I snorted, "Six years! Think of the scandal."

That seemed to throw him for a moment, but he still stubbornly refused to relent. "Blue, please think about this before we do something we can't take back."

Now I laughed, gasping through giggles to the point I pushed Red back so I could sit up. "What? Because I'm some blushing virgin? I assure you, Mr. Cypher, I have done way more with people I cared for way less."

"I'm not sure if I should be flattered or insulted." He mused.

I locked my arms around his neck and pulled him back down on the bed. "Why don't you stop thinking and just kiss me?"

He did, pinning me to the bed in a way that made my toes curl and my nerves tingle with excitement.

I closed my eyes and lost myself in the sensations, the scuff of his cheek against my skin, his calloused fingers on my thigh and the strength of his arms as he held me close.

Afterward, he tried to leave, rising from the bed before the sweat had managed to cool on my skin.

"Stay," I begged, fingers digging into the thick muscle of his arm. He tensed, uncertain, then relaxed and lay back down.

"For as long as you'll have me, I promise."

I smirked against his neck, my nose tracing the edge of his cowl.

"You're the one who told me to never trust a villain," I reminded him.

Red took a breath, wrapping his arms around me and holding me close, but didn't answer.

Chapter Fourteen

My phone buzzed against the nightstand like an angry wasp. I groaned, Red's arm tightening around my waist reflexively as I slapped the top of my alarm clock.

"It is currently 2:37 am," the computerized voice chirped out. I smashed my face into my pillow while the phone continued to vibrate impatiently.

"Ignore it," Red suggested, burrowing his face into my neck, his breath warm and comforting against my skin. "Two am isn't a real time."

I found myself smiling into the soft fabric, which was quickly wiped away as the phone started up again, this time with a cheerful chiming accompaniment, loud and insistent, vibrating against the wood like it was trying to crawl away.

I sighed in exasperation and fumbled for the phone, nearly dropping it as I pressed it to my ear.

"Velvet Walker."

The voice on the other side cracked, breathing hard and panicked. "Hey, er—Velvet, this this Elis Wade, Road Kill."

Instantly, I was wide awake, pushing the blankets off my legs and sitting up in bed. "Road Kill? Where are you? What's wrong?"

"So, there's been a bit of a misunderstanding," Road Kill explained. "One of the gangs I owed money to found me. I didn't start it."

I took the phone from my ear and showed the screen to Red. "What does the caller ID say?"

Red groaned. "City Jail."

I dropped my head into my free hand, massaging the bridge of my nose, before putting the phone back to my ear. "You need me to bail you out?" I surmised.

"I didn't know what else to do. If they put me in holding, the gang bangers are going to fuck me up, and I'm already trying to grow back one of my hands—"

"You're missing a hand?" I squeaked. "Why?"

"I was trying to slide down a fire escape, and it got caught," Road Kill explained as though this was nothing more than a minor inconvenience.

I swung my legs over the side of the bed, the mattress squeaking under me. "I'm on my way. Sit tight." I hung up the phone.

Red was already up and handing me my clothes. "What did the kid do this time?" He asked, while I buttoned my blouse, only to realize it was the one missing a button. I pulled it off and crossed to the dresser.

"Gang stuff," I told him, pulling on the first thing my hands landed on. "He said he didn't start it."

"Did he finish it?" Red inquired.

I snorted, "uncertain. I'll be back in a bit."

"I'll drive you," he offered.

I turned to stare at him, or at least, in his general direction, since I hadn't bothered turning on any lights. "Yeah, let's roll up to a police station with a known felon behind the wheel, great plan."

"I can take off the mask," he offered, and I froze, fully aware of just what he was offering.

"Is that what you want?" I asked him.

He paused, the silence heavy between us.

"It would be dangerous," I mused. "Considering everything."

"I don't want to have secrets from you."

I sat down next to him on the bed and took his face in my hands, my fingers running along the outline of his mask and kissed his lips.

"I'm not saying no," I whispered. "I'm saying not yet."

He nodded, thoughtful. "I'll call you a ride. Are you sure you're okay to go? You just got out of the hospital."

My ribs were still throbbing slightly as I reached for my cane. I took a breath, breathing through the anxiety in my chest. "Can't live in fear," I told him.

He was silent for a moment, floor creaking as he crossed to me. He took me by the shoulders and tenderly kissed my forehead. "That's my girl."

His praise stayed with me through the cab ride. The police station reeked of floor polish and burnt coffee. My boots echoed on the linoleum as I approached the front desk, ID in one hand, cane in the other. I could hear a tired officer shuffling paperwork behind bulletproof glass.

"Name?" the officer asked, voice tired and flat, as I stepped forward

"Velvet Walker. I'm here to post bail for Elis Wade."

A pause. Then a sigh.

"Of course you are."

She muttered something under her breath and tapped at her computer.

"Charges are assault and disturbing the peace. Again. He picked a fight with a local gang and wrecked part of a convenience store. He's got priors, you know."

"Yes," I said. "I'm aware."

Her chair creaked as she leaned forward, her voice dropping into something almost pitying. "Look, Ms. Walker, I saw you on TV. You're a smart woman. I've seen this kid come through here four times in the last two months. Always the same story. Banged up. Half-drunk. Healing too fast for his own good. You really think you can save him?"

"I'm not here to save him," I said, uncomfortable. "Just to keep him from getting himself killed, today."

She sighed again, louder this time, then slid a form across the counter. I signed it, and she buzzed for processing.

Ten minutes later, Road Kill limped out, his footsteps uneven, breath hissing through clenched teeth.

"Velvet," he muttered, trying to sound casual. "Thanks for coming."

I folded my arms. "Got your things?"

He paused, confused. I held my hand out, and after a moment, he slid the strap of his backpack into my hand.

"Good," I told him. "Once we get home, Red Cypher is going to relieve you of any illicit substances."

"What? But—!"

I held up a hand. "Here's the deal. You come home with me, help out, stay clean. No pills, no booze, no fights. You want my help? Earn it. Take it or leave it."

His boots shifted noisily against the laminate as he considered.

"That or you can rot in a holding cell," I told him. "I'm not playing here."

He huffed. "Do you still need people to visit the kids in the hospital?"

"Always," I said.

"Fine," he muttered. "Deal."

I reached and put an arm around him. "Good, come on, we'll stop for food on the way. You must be starving."

His head bobbed up and down, eagerly.

We stepped out into the muggy night, the heavy door thudding shut behind us with a final *clang* that echoed down the empty sidewalk. The air smelled like old rain, pavement, and exhaust. A streetlight buzzed overhead, casting a faint glow I could just make out through the haze.

Road Kill limped beside me, favouring his left leg. I could hear the shallow hitch in his breathing, the quiet grit of pain in his throat he didn't want me to notice.

"You said you lost a hand," I said. "What else?"

"Most of the skin on my left leg. Was dragged for a bit," he muttered. "I'm healing. Just slow. Hurts like hell, though."

I stopped walking, cane tapping the edge of the curb until I found the lip. "Deal still stands. No pills. You break the rules, I walk."

He grumbled something under his breath, but I kept moving, guiding us toward the street where I *hoped* the cab was waiting.

A vehicle idled at the curb ahead, engine humming low and steady.

"That's our ride?" Road Kill asked.

"Only car here," I said, exhaustion falling over me like a blanket, now that the worst was behind us.

He moved ahead of me, boots scuffing the sidewalk. I heard the door open, then his voice, confused and hesitant.

"Velvet?"

"What now?"

He leaned closer, whispering urgently. "Why the hell is Nefarious in the driver's seat?"

I stopped cold, my cane scraping the pavement as I adjusted.

"What?"

"He's just sitting there. Sunglasses on. At night. Like a creep."

From the cab, Nefarious' voice rang out, dry and unimpressed. "I can *hear* you."

I sighed and stepped forward, letting my hand trail along the side of the car until I found the door. I opened it and slid inside.

"Nefarious," I said. "Why?"

"Red said you'd need a ride," he answered flatly. "Figured it was safer than letting you wander around with our favourite human punching bag."

Road Kill climbed into the back, groaning. "I feel *so* loved."

"You should," Nefarious replied, shifting the cab into gear. "This is the nicest thing I've done all week."

As we pulled away from the station, Road Kill slumped beside me, bruised and sulking. As promised, I made Nefarious drive-through for takeout.

The cab ride was long enough for Road Kill to tear through half a burger and complain about the fries being cold. I didn't answer. The familiar rhythm of the city at night was all around us. Distant sirens, the occasional honk, and the soft rumble of passing cars. But underneath it all was the quiet thrum of my own nerves.

Nefarious didn't talk, just drove like he did everything else, smooth, fast and calculating. When the tires hit the cracked driveway, I knew we were home. My cane tapped the curb, then the familiar three steps leading to the porch.

Road Kill climbed out slowly, letting out a grunt as his boots hit the ground. "This is it?"

"Yes," I said. "Don't touch anything."

He followed me up the stairs, carrying the takeout bags.

The door creaked open into the cool air of the hallway.

Then Red's voice, from the kitchen. "About time."

I stepped inside, shutting the door behind Road Kill. "We brought food."

Footsteps on hardwood. I could hear Red's approach, the calm confidence in every step. A pause, then the soft touch of his hand brushing my arm.

"Everything go smoothly?" he asked.

"For jail? Sure," I said.

Road Kill muttered, "I'm standing right here."

"And bleeding on the floor," Red replied coolly.

"I'm not..." Road Kill stopped. "Okay, maybe a little."

I moved toward the kitchen, cane sweeping ahead of me. I could feel the tension building in the air.

Red followed, his voice low. "You sure about this?"

"I don't have to be sure," I said, suddenly so tired I could've fallen asleep right there. "I just have to make it work."

Behind me, Road Kill grumbled as he dropped the food bags on the counter.

I took the first bite of a soggy fry and pointed toward the hallway.

"Bathrooms down the hall. Don't steal anything and try to keep the blood off the floor."

Road Kill sighed. "Noted."

"I'll get you something for your leg," I said, leaving Red and Road Kill to glare at each other. Once in the bathroom, I leaned against the wall, fingers tracing the grooves in the plaster I'd memorized since I was a kid. What would my mother have said if she could see me now? Sleeping with one villain and housing another?

"Blue?" Red's voice startled me out of my musing. He came into the bathroom and wrapped his arms around me, his body warm and solid against me.

"I have half a dozen safe houses we can send him to," he told me earnestly. "You don't have to be responsible for him."

"I am responsible," I told him. "For all of you. I don't get to pick and choose."

We breathed together for a long moment. "You continue to amaze me, Blue. I don't know how you do it."

I huffed into his shoulder, eyes pressed closed to keep the tears from falling. "Honestly? I wasn't given a choice."

Chapter Fifteen

Coming home after a long day to find my home occupied by half a dozen or more supervillains became the norm rather quickly.

"They arrested MidKnight," Road Kill told me, taking the bag of groceries from my arms, as I toed off my shoes.

It had been over four months since I'd been kidnapped, and The Villain Project, as the public had dubbed it, had hit its stride. The local news dedicated a segment to highlighting the week's visits, as well as many villains branching off with their own marketing and social media influence. I'd been featured in *Beyond Powers,* just after getting out of the hospital, to tell the story of my kidnapping and daring rescue. A few weeks later, Emerald Shade had featured me on her podcast, *Shades of Truth,* where she peppered me about my growing relationship with Red Cypher. I'd played coy, to her irritation, but it had still been a fun experience overall.

Despite their outward display of support, the Super Alliance continued to breathe down our necks, enforcing obscure laws and manipulating loopholes, waiting for the one slip-up that would bring our entire tower of cards down on our heads.

"Was he actually arrested, or just in for questioning again?" I asked, skeptical.

"Actually arrested!" Road Kill crowed. A strong, armoured arm wrapped around my waist and I gratefully accepted the kiss Red placed on my lips as we entered the sitting room.

"Unnecessary PDA," Medea called from across the room in a bored tone. Nearby, Hazard muttered in disapproval.

"Who's all here?" I asked, ignoring him. "I bought stuff for Pasta Carbonara, but someone might need to make a run for more fettuccini."

"Save it for tomorrow," Red told me. "I ordered pizza."

I turned my face to focus on him. "You didn't have to do that; I don't mind cooking."

"I know, but we have something that needs to be discussed, and I don't want you to be distracted. "

"Because of the arrest?" I asked, moving to help Road Kill put away the groceries. His help was always appreciated, but he had a habit of putting things away in odd places, and I had trouble finding them afterwards.

"The Supes are floundering," Medea said, her voice sing-song. "The backlash is overwhelming them. People on the internet have been quick to dig up a mountain of condemning information on every single member of the Alliance." From what I could tell, she had draped herself across the sofa, a series of lights floating around her.

"Medea, please," I pleaded, "it's hard enough to see as it is."

"Apologies." The lights went out, though not without leaving an unpleasant afterimage on my retinas.

"Not every member," Hazard bit out. "They've yet to dig up anything on Black Bullet. Rat bastard is like the second coming."

I frowned, unsettled by something in his tone, but remained silent while Road Kill and I packed away the last of the groceries.

"If we can dig up dirt on him, the Super Alliance will crumble." Hazard went on, "but the fool is bulletproof."

"Of course he is," Medea said, confused. "He also shoots lightning and punches through walls."

"I'm meant figuratively, idiot girl," Hazard snarled.

Medea scoffed. "Big talk from the fool who was nearly arrested robbing a pharmacy last week."

I whirled on the two of them, aghast. "What? When did this happen?"

Hazard growled while Medea talked over him, unconcerned. "Wednesday afternoon. Idiot went after a mom-and-pop shop for their entire supply of Sudafed."

"I had a migraine," Hazard said, unconcerned.

"That's bullshit and you know it." I snapped, "Are you seriously cooking meth in your spare time?"

"Do I look like some low-life junkie?" Hazard scoffed. "MidKnight told you Black Bullet was after Oblivion. I'm going to figure it out first."

"How?" Red asked, dubious. "On a wish and a prayer? If the researchers working for Titan haven't been able to figure it out, I doubt you'll be able to do it in your one-room bunker."

"Besides, it's just plain reckless, Hazard," I told him. "What happened to visiting Erica Morrison in hospice?"

Hazard waved a dismissive hand, which was easy to track thanks to the bright neon yellow of his suit. "Supers were staking out the hospital. I had to reschedule."

I took a long breath through my nose, blood rising. "As your attorney, I have to advise you to turn yourself in."

This was the wrong thing to say. The accompanying silence was thick and heavy, like rapids against a dam that was slowly falling apart.

"You're not my attorney," Hazard said. His voice dropped, bitter and tight. "You're just some blind idealist who thinks she can tame monsters by making them sandwiches."

"Say that again," Red demanded, voice low and sharp.

Hazard ignored him. "And you—" his footsteps circled, fast, aggressive, "You used to be the worst of us, Cypher. You were a nightmare, blacking out power grids, hacking into government mainframes. Now you're doing *dishes*."

"I like dishes," Red replied coolly. "They keep my hands busy."

Medea snorted. "He's not wrong. You're practically suburban."

"You want to go back to blood and headlines?" I asked. "Be my guest. But don't come into my home and spit on the only thing keeping us alive. One mistake, one, and everything we built comes crashing down."

"Your home," Hazard spat, mocking. "Because you're so much better than us. Because you get to tell us what to do and how to behave. Make us smile for the camera like tigers on display.

"You're soft," he spat. "You all are. Cypher's not Red Cypher anymore; he's playing house. Road Kill's sober. Nefarious hasn't threatened to dissect anyone in *weeks*. And you."

He stepped towards me, filling my pinhole vision with his girth. "You think you're leading us, but you're just a well-dressed leash."

Red was in between us in an instant, pushing me backwards. "You want to insult me, fine. You want to insult her? Say it again."

Hazard's nostrils flared. "The Syndicate doesn't care about your personal growth. They want results. They want destruction. Chaos. You think they'll sit around and wait while you play lawyer and host dinner parties in your dead mom's kitchen?"

"Don't talk about my mother," I snapped.

The room went quiet.

Medea's nails tapped a pattern on the wooden furniture. "Yikes."

Road Kill muttered, "He's not wrong. About the Syndicate watching."

Nefarious tilted his head. "It's not a question of *if*. Just how long until they decide we're not useful anymore?"

"Pizza time!" Dr. Nefarious announced, stepping into the room. The scent of cheese and pepperoni wafted around him. His steps faltered as he took in the tense atmosphere.

"Er, what did I miss?"

A long, silent moment passed, the tension thick as molasses.

Finally, I swallowed, gathering my courage. "Hazard, I think you should leave."

"Gladly," he spat. His heavy boots thumped against the floor. "I'll be back when the Syndicate decides to do away with you and your pets for good." The door slammed behind him, causing the pictures on the walls to shake.

"Well fuck him," Nefarious said, completely unbothered. "As long as the Supes are unhappy and flailing, I'm happy."

His steps were light as he crossed to the kitchen to put down the pizza. "I met with Tommy yesterday for his three-month scan. The tumour is more than half reduced in size, and he's got most of the mobility on his right side back. His mother kissed me! I've never felt so rewarded. She's recommended three more children for my services."

I took a breath, still shaky from the encounter with Hazard. "Will you be able to help them?" I asked, sitting down at the table. Red placed a slice of pizza in front of me and rubbed my shoulders comfortingly.

"Prospects look promising, but I'll need to conduct a few tests," Nefarious told us through a mouthful of cheese.

"As long as none of them decide to sell you out," Medea quipped from just behind me. I was able to track her arm as she reached over my shoulder for a slice of pizza.

"Bah," Nefarious waved a hand. "I'm saving their children. It is in their best interest to keep quiet."

"As welcome as your news is, Nefarious," Red said. "I think we should get to the matter at hand."

"The matter at hand?" I asked, picking at my own slice of pizza. "I didn't realize this was an official meeting of... whatever the hell we are."

"Blind Justice and her collection of criminals?" Road Kill suggested.

I cringed. "Oh God, no."

"The Reformed Villain collective?" Nefarious mused around a mouthful of cheese.

Medea chuckled. "Reformed might be reaching, considering what I was up to last night."

"I don't want to know," I declared, mildly hysterical. "Please, allow me my ignorance."

"Everyone," Red insisted. "Listen. Hazard wasn't just blowing smoke out his ass about the Syndicate. They've been in contact with us."

That got everyone's attention. The room grew eerily still and silent. Nefarious swallowed, and the sounds seemed to echo in the small space.

"When?" Medea demanded.

"Just after Velvet received the invitation."

"What invitation?" I asked.

Medea scoffed. "You don't know? You've been invited to the annual Super Alliance Charity Ball! I mean, really, what do you pay that assistant for?"

"What?" I gaped. "Please tell me you're joking."

"Casey received the invitation this morning, and the Twilight Syndicate contacted me about it just after," Red explained. "They have a job for us, and I think it's in all of our best interests."

"I thought the Syndicate didn't like me." I reminded him. "Hazard seemed convinced it wouldn't be long before they called for my head on a plate."

"Oh, that was before you became of use to them, my darling." Medea crooned, her hand sliding gently over my arm. I jumped, not realizing she'd remained so close.

"So what?" I asked. "They want me to attend the ball? What for?"

"They want *us* to attend the ball." Red clarified. "The ball is held at the Super Alliance headquarters, home of their state-of-the-art mainframe. The Syndicate is practically salivating at the chance of getting a hold of even a tenth of that database."

"They have to be anticipating this?" I pointed out. "They're not just going to let me walk in with Red Cypher on my arm and look the other way while you go snooping."

"I won't be Red Cypher," Red explained. "I've got a few aliases that should fly under the radar. Plus, we'll have Medea and Nefarious working as backup to alleviate suspicion. Hazard was supposed to be included, but we'll have to do without him now."

"Phff," Nefarious said, sending bits of spittle over me. "We're better off without that hot head."

"I don't know you guys," I lamented, pushing away from the table. "It's a really big place, unfamiliar surroundings with a huge crowd."

"I'll be with you the entire time," Red assured me. "We're going to try and set up a wireless tap to draw the data out over time."

"Come on, Velvet." Medea persuaded. "What girl doesn't want to attend a fancy ball, wearing a gorgeous dress, with a handsome man on her arm?"

I swallowed and murmured under my breath.

"Pardon?"

I sighed and lifted my head. "I don't own a dress."

"What?" Medea gasped. "Now you are joking?"

"I don't wear them!" I told her. "I don't like them. My mother had some, but I gave them to charity after she died."

"This is a worse crime than even I could have committed." I heard fingers tapping on a screen.

"What are you doing?" I demanded.

"Contacting Casey to cancel your appointments for tomorrow. She'll take you to get measurements. I have a fantastic dress maker you're going to see as soon as possible."

"Better take her for hair and makeup as well," Nefarious suggested. "Maybe have her nails painted. I go to the one on Fifth and Main. Kathy, who works there, is a genius, and that's saying something coming from me."

"It's not just that!" I stated, flustered. "I can't be an accomplice in a data heist. I shouldn't be hearing any of this."

It was as though a bubble burst, filling the room with tension once again.

"So, are you going to make us all turn ourselves in?" Road Kill asked, hesitantly. I'd almost forgotten he was there.

"No!" I squeaked, and then with more force. "No, of course not. I mean, technically, as your attorney, I have to recommend you do the right thing, but I'm not going to make you do anything you don't want to. I would expect the same courtesy from all of you."

I glared at them, features hard.

"We're not asking you to commit a crime," Red told me. "You'd never even touch a keyboard. All you'd have to do is smile, shake hands, distract a few capes..."

"No," I said, firm. "It's one thing to organize visits and sell merchandise. Knowingly helping commit an illegal act? That crosses a line."

"Even after what MidKnight did?" Road Kill asked.

I crossed my arms. "I won't stoop to his level."

"Or ours?" Medea huffed. "Sure, you break bread with us, but you're still above us."

"That's not what I meant." I groaned.

"No, no," Medea said, her figure shifting across the room, heels clicking as she strolled towards the door. "I understand completely."

"Yeah, I think I'll grab some slices for the road, if you don't mind." Without waiting for a response, Nefarious piled several pizza slices on top of each other before heading after Medea, door slamming closed behind them.

I buried my head in my hands. "That's not what I meant!" I pleaded.

"What did you mean then?" Road kill demanded. "What are we even doing here if you're just going to use us and then hand us over to the Supes when you're done with us?"

I was on my feet in an instant, hands clenched into fists at my sides. "I did not say that. I would never turn you over to the Supes. I hate Black Bullet and the Super Alliance as much as you do!"

"But you won't help us bring them down," Road Kill pointed out. "Because you think you're better than us."

"That's enough," Red snapped. "Road Kill, go to your room."

"Fuck you, man," Road Kill spat. "You're not my dad."

"Then take a walk." Red spat right back. "Just make yourself scarce. Velvet and I need to talk."

"Whatever," Road Kill said, and I tracked him as he stormed out the door.

I spoke before Red got the chance, still seething. "If this was your plan all along, then you might as well leave too."

"My plan?" Red asked, taking my hand and gently straightening each tense finger one at a time, the knuckles still ached slightly from when MidKnight had broken them.

"Win me over, make me fall for you and then rope me into your diabolical plan," I said, tears burning the corners of my eyes.

Red sighed. "Falling for you was never part of the plan, Velvet."

I sniffed. Tears began to fall. "Rule number one," I bit out.

"I still stand by that," he told me. "But if I'd wanted to trick you into helping us, I wouldn't have told you about the plan to begin with. I could have just escorted you to the ball, completely unaware, but I didn't because you're part of the team."

I covered my face, sobbing into my hands. Red's arms came around my shoulders supporting me.

"Listen, I'm not saying we're the good guys, far from it," he said finally, voice low enough the words felt like they belonged only to me. "We're the villains and we're gonna do what villains do."

"That's not helping your case," I muttered against his chest.

"I'm not making a case, Blue. I'm reminding you of where you are." His hand came up to brush the hair from my face. "You've invited us into your home, eat with us, risk your neck for us. You've seen what Supers do to people they don't control, and

128

you've seen what the Syndicate does to the ones they can't use."

I swallowed hard, the truth sitting heavy in my chest.

"I know we've talked a lot about who I am behind the mask." He went on, and I blinked, confused at the sudden shift. "I know we've decided it's safer I keep it for now, but I need you to know I am who I am because I saw through the façade of the Supes. Just like you, I saw what they really were, and I vowed to make the whole world see it too. Not just for me, but for everyone who's ever been taken in by their act and then had their dreams shattered."

"People like Sam Hall?" I asked. He didn't reply, so I went on. "I went to his funeral, and his father couldn't even look at me."

Red let out a long breath. "I'm sure it wasn't you he was angry with."

"I let down that little boy, Red."

"Black Bullet let down that boy, and he keeps doing it. I've been keeping track. Requests for visits with Black Bullet have gone down twenty percent since the Villain Project began. Do you know how many he's actually attended?"

I didn't want to know. I had to know. "How many?"

"Three," he told me. "Out of a possible fifty-six."

It wasn't my fault, but I still felt responsible somehow. A narcissistic asshole was parading around in the guise of a superhero, lying to the public and dashing children's hopes and dreams.

Red tipped my chin up just enough for me to feel the heat of his gaze. "It's only the tip of the iceberg, Blue. There is serious corruption in the Super Alliance. Things are lingering in Black Bullet's closet that would make MidKnight look like the Dalai Lama in comparison."

"Like Oblivion?" I guessed. "He's not going to let that go anytime soon."

"And if he gets his hands on it?" Red went on. "Suddenly, he is the sole decider on who has powers and who doesn't."

The air between us felt like a wire pulled tight.

"It's your decision if you want to help us or not," he said, voice like smoke and steel, "but if you do, then you walk into that ball on our side. And whatever happens, happens to all of us."

The thing was, I already knew the answer. I'd known for a while.

My fingers curled against his armour, pressing close.

"Fine," I sighed. "But I'm not trying on a bunch of stupid frilly dresses."

Red laughed and kissed the top of my head. "Don't worry, I have that completely covered."

Chapter Sixteen

The dress was made of crushed blue velvet, of course

The fabric draped around me in layers, weighing me down. With my pinhole vision, I wasn't able to get the full effect of my impromptu makeover. My head felt lighter after a proper trim, the ends curled in a way that tickled my cheeks. Casey assured me the makeup was very natural-looking.

I assumed anyone else would feel beautiful, all dolled up and spoiled. I just felt sick. The dress reminded me more of a Halloween costume than a formal gown.

"You look stunning," Red told me as he held the door to the car open. He'd exchanged his scarlet uniform for a dark suit and deep black hood, face completely obscured in shadow.

"I'll take your word for it," I told him a bit more spitefully than I meant to as I settled myself into the seat.

"Nervous?" he asked as we pulled out.

"They're going to figure out something is going on." I blurted out in a panicked rush. "There's a ton of security, and like, how many supers will be there? This is insane."

"You have nothing to worry about," Red assured me. "We've got everything planned out to the smallest detail. Medea and Hazard are already in place."

"Hazard?" I just about choked. "After the stunt, he pulled back at the house?"

"He and The Syndicate had words," Red explained casually. "He's being generously rewarded for adding his expertise to the plan."

I took a slow, deep breath. "The Syndicate has more faith in him than I do."

"Me too," Red agreed. "But they've never held my opinion in high regard. Don't worry about Hazard. All you need to do is stick with me and look pretty."

I sighed, through lips sticky with balm. "I'll do my best."

The lights outside the Super Alliance headquarters were too much for my eyes, and I was forced to let Red guide me down the improvised red carpet, while photographers blinded me even further with their unrelenting camera flashes.

"Ms. Walker? A word?"

"Serena Thomas," Red whispered, tugging me to a stop. "Channel Five News."

A microphone squealed in front of me, and a figure, whom I assumed was Serena, stepped in front of us.

"Hi," I said, awkwardly.

"Ms. Walker, it must be such an honour to have been invited to the Super Alliance's charity ball this year."

"Actually," I said, pulling at the skirt of my dress. "I'm finding it a bit overwhelming."

Serena gave an awkward chortle. "Yes, I suppose anyone would find all of this intimidating, especially considering your disability."

It felt like a slight, and I took it as one. "Actually, lately I've been feeling like I'm the only one seeing the world clearly."

Serena cleared her throat, uncomfortable. "Who is your guest this evening?" She asked.

"Sooth Sayer," Red answered. "Reformed villain. I work for Ms. Walker."

Serena clamped onto this new revelation with a vice-like grip. "Oh, wonderful. The lengths Ms. Walker has been taking to reform the supervillain community are something the Super Alliance has been praising."

"Oh well, thank fucking God the Super Alliance is happy," I muttered under my breath, absolutely done with this farce of an interview.

"Well, we'd better let you go," Red said as he gripped my arm and tugged me away. "Looks like Black Bullet just arrived."

This appeared to be the case as I could hear the crowd of interviewers and paparazzi calling out to the superhero, cameras flashing in my periphery and making my head hurt.

"I've never made it a secret how much I like your sharp tongue," Red said as we continued into Super Alliance headquarters. "However, perhaps there is a time and place?"

"She was being a bitch," I told him.

"Oh, no argument, but we usually try not to insult people during undercover missions."

I rolled my eyes. "Fine, I'll focus on looking pretty."

"You do it so well," Red told me.

The marble lobby echoed every heel strike and polite laugh. I didn't need full sight to sense the grandeur. Every voice sounded small against the cavernous ceilings, and the mingling perfumes and colognes layered themselves together like armour.

The ballroom proper was worse. Strings and piano filled the air with their lazy, uninspired notes. Chandelier's glittered with diamond light, stabbing little white ghosts into the edges of my sight.

"Don't forget to smile," Red murmured, his arm steady around mine.

I pulled my lips back just enough to show teeth. The smile of a woman enduring a bad dentist.

Red's grip tightened ever so slightly. "And here comes the man himself, heading straight for us."

I groaned. "We should have hit the bar first."

"Ms. Walker," Black Bullet said, filling my vision with his smug face. "So glad you could make it."

"Black Bullet," I smiled. "Thank you so much for the invitation."

"Of course!" he said, his voice over the top as though trying to draw attention to his generosity. "I wouldn't dream of leaving out someone so instrumental to mending the rift between heroes and villains."

"I suspect the rift was by design." I smirked. He didn't take the bait.

"How are you holding up after all that unpleasantness?" he asked, though it was clear from his tone that he did not care. "I do hope there was no lasting damage."

"That would have been unfortunate," I snarked. "Especially since it was your guard dog who almost took my head off."

"MidKnight has been removed from active duty and reprimanded for that infraction." Black Bullet's voice was low and firm. "We did issue an apology."

"Oh, yes, I really appreciated you giving him a slap on the wrist and saying you were so sorry." I could feel Red's disapproving stare, but I found I couldn't stop myself. Blood pounded in my ears, and my face was aflame.

Black Bullet was silent for a long moment, and I prayed he would just leave well enough alone; instead, he gripped my arm and tugged me forcefully away from Red.

"Come, dance with me," he insisted.

"No, thank you." I spat out from between clenched teeth. He ignored me.

"You don't mind me stealing her away for a moment, do you? Black Bullet asked, definitely directed at Red.

"Er—" Was all Red managed to get out before I was being whisked away to the stuffy, crowded dance floor.

His gloved hands were vices on my body as we swayed awkwardly amongst the partygoers. Their stares prickled against me like hot needles.

"You are playing a very dangerous game, Velvet." Black Bullet told me under his breath. "You have no idea the strings I've had to pull to keep you from having an, let's say, unfortunate accident."

I was shocked, my mouth hanging open like a fish. "So what? You want me to thank you for not having me assassinated when your first attempt failed?"

"MidKnight acted of his own—"

"Oh, fuck off, everyone saw the video. What do you want with the formula for Oblivion?"

"It's none of your concern," Black Bullet said. "Unless there's something you're holding back?'

"No," I fumed. "And even if I did, I wouldn't tell you."

Black Bullet sighed in frustration. "You're so quick to fall on your sword, yet you fail to realize I hold all the cards here. I always have. The Villain project only exists because I allow it. You've been walking the edge of this knife for long enough. It's time for you to realize you have no power here."

"They're never going to work for you," I reminded him. "The villains are always going to have their own agenda, and number one on the docket is taking you and the Super Alliance down."

Black Bullet let out a harsh laugh. "They can try. Every failed attempt just boosts our ranking in the eyes of the public. I hope you enjoy the rest of your evening, Ms. Walker."

He let go of me and walked away into the crowd, leaving me stranded amongst the sea of people. My hand went for my cane, but Red had been holding it. My heart beat a panicked rhythm as a dancing couple bumped into me, and I nearly stumbled to the floor.

"Watch it," someone snapped and angry tears burned my eyes as I stood frozen in the middle of the dance floor, humiliated.

Then gentle hands settled onto my shoulders, leading me carefully through the dancing couples. "You okay, Blue?" Red asked.

"Fucking asshole," I sniffed. "He left me there on purpose. He's trying to prove he's always the one in control."

"Not for long," Red promised me. "We've got the location of the server room. Once the speeches start, I'll slip out and access the mainframe."

"And I stand here and look pretty?" I guessed.

"And keep an ear out for any wrinkles."

"Aye, Captain," I sighed.

He led me to the back of the ballroom, where a corridor branched off down a service hallway. We waited as applause thundered through the ballroom and the chairman of Titan Global took the stand, launching into a self-gratifying speech about all the things Titan did to make themselves look good in the eyes of the public.

Red's hand slipped from mine, and I watched him leave by feeling the emptiness at my side. The hum of the crowd reformed around his absence. I could feel the shape of him gone from my periphery. My skin registered the vacancy like an ache.

I tried to stand tall and not fidget. I needed to play my part, the quiet face in the corner. I wrapped my arms around my waist, and my fingers brushed over something that made my other senses buzz to life.

I lifted a single hair from my dress, my mind instantly shuffling through my collection of chemical compounds. After a moment, I knew where I'd encountered this specific DNA before.

On the night of my mother's murder.

"Possible security breach in level two. Thought I saw someone near the server room."

I jumped at the clipped static of the radio. A security guard nearby responded instantly.

"Cameras caught one of the guests heading that way. Request backup."

I was moving before I'd fully made up my mind, the tapping of my cane echoing down the empty hall. I made my way to the far end, where a stairwell led down to the second level. The door banged closed behind me as I navigated the steep staircase.

The second level was dark. Concrete instead of marble. I took a moment to listen, but there didn't seem to be any sign of life. I started forward, the sharp scent of chemicals and burning metal filling my nose.

"Red?" I whispered, placing my hand against the wall and feeling each doorway as I passed. They were few and far between, though the hum of electronics became more distinct as I went on.

Finally, after five doors, the sixth opened easily under my hand. The sound swallowed me, racks of computers humming like a mechanical heartbeat.

"Blue?" Red said, startled. "What are you doing here?"

"Security is on its way," I told him. "We need to go."

"I need five more minutes." The keyboard clicked so quickly under his fingers that it was almost a hum.

"Actually, your time is up."

I jumped, skidding further into the room, my cane held in front of me like a sword. Black Bullet filled the doorway, the vibration of the servers and computer systems dimming at his presence, his shadow dragging the light from the room.

"It was only a matter of time." Black Bullet's voice was full of triumph. "I knew the lure of the mainframe would be too much to resist, and now I've got you. The villains exposed for what they've always been, criminals through and through."

But we'd prepared for this. Behind me, the computer clicked as Red pulled the drive from the mainframe. Alarms began to blare overhead as smoke started to fill the room.

Red grabbed my arm and yanked me back, further into the server room, the air hot and metallic.

"Don't move," Red hissed in my ears as Black Bullet stumbled blindly after us. Electricity hummed in the air, and the smell of ozone hit me full in the face just as a nearby computer exploded, sending flames tall enough to lick the ceiling.

"Come, quick!" I was pulled upright, my feet tripping over my long skirts and unseen vents and wires until the air shifted and we were out in the hallway once more.

"Get back here!" Black Bullet howled from somewhere back in the chaos.

"No thanks," Red quipped, darting off with me in tow."

"You can't run forever!"

A door banged open to our right, and I flinched in anticipation of an attack.

"Way to blow the plan sky high!" Nefarious scolded.

"Just a minor hiccup," Red assured him, "The Dead Channel is in place."

"A lot of good it'll do," Nefarious reported. "They've initiated lockdown procedures. Medea is keeping Black Bullet busy for now, but it's only a matter of time till he breaks free."

"We planned for this," Red assured him. A heavy door clanged open, and we entered into a drafty stairwell, Red and Nefarious's boots thudding against the stairs as we ascended, my impractical high heels tripping me up as I struggled to keep pace. Another door banged below us, heavy footsteps pouring out onto the stairs. Radio's crackled, voices barking orders.

"They're coming," Nefarious hissed.

We continued upwards, security in hot pursuit. On the next landing, Red ducked into the doorway, pulling me tight against him. I could feel the sharp hammer of his pulse beneath his armour. He shifted forward, blocking me from view, his suit buzzing as he readied a weapon, the safety clicking off, followed by the low hum of suppressed energy, the air filling with the scent of heated metal.

And then, a woman's familiar laughter echoed around us.

"Medea," I whispered, relief flooding through me.

The sounds around us fractured. The sudden shouts of men and then the deafening crash of gunfire, glass shattering, radios screeching. Miraculously, none of it was directed at us.

"What are they shooting at?" Red demanded.

"Phantoms," Medea's voice was right beside me, cutting through the chaos. "Move! I can't hold it for long."

"Where's Hazard?" Red demanded.

"Took off as soon as the alarms sounded," Medea said, venom filling her voice. "Good riddance."

In one quick, fluid motion, Red scooped me into his arms, my dress bunching around me like a cocoon. He barreled forward, Medea and Nefarious on his heels. My world became sound and motion. The slam of a door, the hollow echo of concrete beneath us, the cold rush of air as another set of doors opened.

A car engine roared to life, and gentle hands guided me into the backseat, leather creaking under my weight. Red slid in beside me, and the vehicle lurched forward, tires screaming against the pavement.

Sirens echoed in the distance as a cold realization rushed over me like ice water.

"Oh God," I gasped. "I'm a wanted criminal."

"You say it like it's a bad thing," Medea pouted. Red wrapped his arms around me, holding me tight.

"Fuck, Velvet," he said, completely distraught. "I'm so sorry."

"Keep it together, Cypher." Nefarious barked from the driver's seat. "Contact Road Kill and get him to meet us at the safe house. They'll hit the house first."

"My house?" I breathed, "No, they can't. I have to go home!"

"It's not you're home anymore, Lipchen," Medea told me sadly. "It was always going to end this way."

"Bullshit," Red snapped. "I should never have dragged you into this."

"Dragged me?" I spat, heat flooding my chest. "You didn't drag me anywhere!"

"Enough," Nefarious snapped, cutting us off. "Save the lovers' spat for later. We need clear heads. Let Road Kill know we're about thirty minutes out. I've got to make sure we're not followed."

"Done," Medea said.

"He knew," Red muttered, his grip on me tightening.

Medea's head shot up, the streetlights strobing behind her, making her formless and indistinct. "What do you mean?"

Red's throat worked, swallowing hard as he chose his words. "Bullet. He wasn't surprised to find us there. He expected it. It was a setup from the start."

The car went silent, save for the whine of the engines and the wail of the distant sirens. My stomach dropped like a stone.

"I guess they were done waiting for us to make a mistake," I said. "They needed to force our hand."

"But the Syndicate were the ones who wanted us to hack the mainframe in the first place." Medea protested.

"The Syndicate has always been playing 3D chess while we're all stuck on tic-tac-toe," Nefarious grumbled. "Who knows what their real objective was?"

"I always thought they just like to watch the world burn," Medea murmured.

I pressed my forehead against Red's shoulder, heart hammering. My house. My career. My life. All of it was ash already, and the world hadn't even seen the flames yet.

Chapter Seventeen

Reports from the Super Alliance's Annual Charity Ball cite Velvet Walker, also known as *Blind Justice*, the so-called *Villain Wrangler* and head of the controversial Villain Project, funded by the Miracle Network, has fled custody after being caught conspiring with known supervillains in an attempt to steal confidential Alliance files.

"Officials warn Walker is considered dangerous and complicit in ongoing threats to public safety. Sources within the Alliance say she used her position to enable criminal activity under the guise of rehabilitation. We go now to the Super Alliance Headquarters for a statement from Black Bullet—"

"Ug," Medea groaned. "Turn it off, Nefarious. I think we've heard quite enough from that bastard."

The car pulled into the shadow of a building, rumbling as a garage door rolled up, and we drove inside, the door closing behind us.

The air changed as the doors opened. Damp and metallic, tinged with pigeons and stale smoke. I could smell rust and oil, the ghost of machinery.

"Holy shit, you're alive!" Road Kill's voice was a cross between disbelief and amazement. "They've got at least five blocks around the headquarters quartered off. How did you make it out?"

"By the skin of our teeth," Medea told him, each click of her boots echoing in the large space. "This is you're safehouse, Red? A condemned factory?"

"It's out of the way, and the owner is listed as a holding company that only exists on paper," Red told them, helping me from the car. "No one should be able to track us here."

The others' voices rose and fell, but I couldn't make out the words over the hum of the overhead lights. The pitch scratched at the back of my teeth, jagged as glass. My breath came short, and my cane tapped uselessly against the concrete until Red caught my wrist.

"You're trembling," he whispered, wrapping his arms around me.

"I'm fine," I lied. My stomach was in knots; it lurched as though we were still in the car, jolting through traffic.

"You don't look fine," Medea muttered. "Make her sit down, Red, she's liable to collapse."

"I said I'm fine," I snapped a little too loudly. My voice echoed over our heads, my words thrown back at me in a mocking litany.

"You don't have to be fine," Red told me softly. "You don't have to be strong all the time."

I was about to tell him that falling apart would serve no one, when a sharp crack filled the air. The garage door groaned under the pressure of something on the other side.

"Fuck, how did they find us?" Red cursed. Another bang and the door folded in on itself with a mighty crash.

"Go!" Red shoved me towards the shadows between the hulking machinery, his voice raw with panic. "Quick, up towards the roof."

Boots hammered the floor and clanged against the metal of the stairs as we rushed upward, my dress hampering me at every turn. My heart raced as our pursuer closed in, fast, disciplined, coordinated. The kind of steps that never stumble.

We made it to the catwalks hanging high over the warehouse. Red held my hand, guiding me blindly after the others, when there was an echoing crack and shriek of a grappling line. A figure flew through the air, landing with a clang onto the catwalk, knocking me backwards.

"Velvet!" Red shouted as the figure loomed over me. The smell of leather, steel and smoke hit me before his voice did.

"End of the line," MidKnight growled.

I gripped my cane tight and swung it up at him, too slow. Pain bloomed white-hot across my ribs as something heavy slammed into me. My breath tore free in a scream I didn't recognize as mine.

"Get away from her!" Red growled, lunging forward. The clash of bodies rattled the entire catwalk, a hollow groan reverberating through the steel beams. My ears rang with the impact.

Red grunted as MidKnight drove him into the railing. Metal shrieked, bolts strained. My heart seized; the drop beneath us felt like it was already pulling me down.

I struggled to my feet, brandishing my cane uselessly in front of me, swinging wildly in the direction of the fight. By sheer luck, I connected with something solid. MidKnight snarled, furious and animalistic. A hand caught my cane out of the air and ripped it from my hands, before swinging it brutally into the side of my head.

I dropped against the guardrail, pain overwhelming me as I struggled to stay conscious.

Red roared, the sound ripping through the air. He threw himself at MidKnight, fists like hammers, striking him over and over until the steel groaned. I smelled the hot tang of blood, sharp and iron-rich, spilling across the catwalk.

MidKnight gurgled, his boots clanging against the grating as he tried to rise. Red hauled him upwards, the two bodies flailing together in one incomprehensible mass, before MidKnight was thrown over the guardrail. His surprised shout cut off abruptly as he slammed into the concrete below.

The buzzing of the industrial lights filled the silence. My chest heaved as I clutched the railing, every nerve screaming.

Red rushed to my side, gathering me up in his arms.

I swallowed, tasting blood in the back of my mouth. "Is he dead?"

Red's breath hitched, then steadied. "Yes."

I closed my eyes, the pain in my head throbbing with every heartbeat.

"Good."

Chapter Eighteen

Glass shattered, the sound sharp enough to make me flinch. A rush of warm air washed over me as someone, Medea probably, kicked the broken pane out of the door.

"Inside," Nefarious barked. "Hurry!"

Red cradled me to his chest, the stench of blood clinging to my dress. My head pounded, my side burned with every breath, sharp and shallow, like someone had wired barbed hooks into my abdomen.

"Here!" Nefarious called out, the smell of antiseptic and floor polish filling my nose. "Put her on the bed."

Each step sent a jolt through me, fire threading through my body until spots burst across what little vision I had left. Red set me down on a medical bed, paper crinkling beneath me. I bit down on a whimper, but it slipped through anyway.

"She's guarding her side," Red muttered, voice frayed at the edges. "That's not ribs."

"I know where my ribs are." I hissed. "This is deeper. Hurts like hell when I breathe too much."

Nefarious' hands were on me, clinical and cold. The neck of my dress was pulled tight, and scissors snipped through the fabric. Gooseflesh prickled over the newly exposed skin.

"Classic spleen shot," he said, his fingers pressing a burning path down my side. "If it's bleeding, you're screwed."

"I'm guessing you didn't pack any of your magic nanites," I moaned.

"You guessed correctly."

Red hovered so close I could feel the heat of him. "How do we check?"

"X-ray," Nefarious said flatly. "Assuming this dump still has one. Otherwise..." He trailed off, already shoving away from the bed. "Look for imaging equipment."

Boots thundered across linoleum. Drawers slammed. Doors banged. A few minutes later, Medea's voice floated back from somewhere outside the exam room. "Got something. Not an X-ray. Portable ultrasound."

"That'll do," Nefarious snapped.

The machine wheezed as it powered on. The screen glowed pale green. Cold gel smeared across my skin and made me hiss. The wand was pressed firmly against my side. I clenched my jaw as the pressure sent lightning through my ribs.

"Hold still," Nefarious ordered.

The grainy screen flickered with shapes I couldn't see. Silence fell, thick and oddly weighted.

"Well?" I demanded, impatient. "Is my spleen bleeding or not?"

Nefarious didn't answer right away. The probe shifted lower, his breath catching.

"What?" Red's voice cracked. "What is it?"

Another silence, broken only by the machine's steady hum. Then Nefarious exhaled through his nose, voice tight. "Your spleen is fine, just a bad bruise. But Velvet, you're pregnant."

My breath caught, the shock enough to block out the pain. For a moment, the words didn't even make sense; it was just noise. Pregnant.

My hands went to my stomach on instinct.

"The fight. MidKnight hit me." My voice cracked. "Is it okay?"

Nefarious adjusted the probe and clicked a dial on the machine. "Hang on."

The wand pressed lower, slower this time. I was too numb to feel anything. A baby, my baby. Was it too late? Did I already lose them before we'd even said hello?

Red was there, taking my hand and running his fingers through my hair. He pressed his lips to my brow as we listened in tense silence to the gurgling whirl, whirl, whirl of the ultrasound.

"Oh God," I whispered, fearing the worst and then, miraculously, a heartbeat, strong and undeniable.

I burst into tears, sobbing uncontrollably into my hand.

"Tough little bastard," Medea cheered. "Well done, Velvet!"

"Looks like you're about twenty-two weeks," Nefarious explained. "No sign of placental abruption. The fetus is healthy and not the least bit shy. Want to know the gender?"

"Uh…" Red faltered.

I blurted out, "Yes!" Desperate now to know everything I could about the tiny little stranger inside me.

"Little boy," Nefarious told us.

Red pulled me close and buried his face in my hair, his body trembling against me.

"Promise me you won't name the poor thing, purple," Medea warned. Red and I burst into laughter, which bordered on hysterics.

Nefarious huffed. "Well, now that the dramatics are over, that head wound could use a few sutures. The rest of you can stock up on supplies. Medea, Road Kill go through every cupboard and gather medical supplies, prenatal vitamins, first aid, the works."

"There are some extra scrubs in here, Velvet," Medea told me. "That dress is a lost cause."

"Oddly enough, I'm not broken up about it," I made the mistake of trying to move myself off the table. I winced and jerked back down, feeling like I might throw up.

"I can try and heal you a bit," Road Kill offered, but I waved him off.

"No use for two of us to be injured," I told him. "I'm fine. The doctor will take care of me."

Once my head was stitched, Nefarious left Red to help me change, while he scavenged for more supplies.

We hobbled to the washroom, which was well-lit, making it easy to navigate. Red helped me up onto the countertop and pulled the remains of the dress over my head. He ran the water, wetting a towel and wiping the blood from my face. I placed a hand over my stomach, trying to feel the tiny life there.

"Should we talk about the elephant in the room?" Red asked, his hands gentle as he cleaned my face.

"I know I'm pregnant," I said, my voice echoing over the tiles. "But it'll be a while before I'm the size of an elephant."

He sighed, not reacting to the joke. "Pregnant," he whispered.

"Yeah," I whispered back,

"You want to keep it." It was a statement, not a question.

"You don't?" I asked, fear bubbling up in my chest. I rushed into this too fast. It was too much,

"Velvet," he said, one hand propped against the mirror as he dropped his face into the other. "I am fucking terrified."

"What are you scared of?" I demanded.

"What I've always been scared of," he said. "Losing the people I love. It wasn't enough that I pulled you into all of this, uprooted your life, nearly got you killed; now I've gone and brought another innocent into it. All of this, and you don't even know who I am; you've never seen my face. How is any of this fair?"

"Life isn't fair," I told him, and he scoffed. "It's true. I told you, I don't need to see your face to know who you are."

"Velvet," he began, unconvinced, but I cut him off.

"You're the man who protected me from MidKnight," I told him. "Who gave me every chance to get out of this. You've protected me at every corner. You've held me and comforted me and made me feel human again at the lowest point in my life. That's who you are, that's who my child's father is. That is the man I love."

"Love," he breathed. "You love me."

"Of course I do," I told him. "And I know you'll protect us."

"And if I can't?" he demanded. "If this all goes sideways and I lose everything all over again."

I frowned. "What do you mean?"

But he was already shaking his head, his hand slipping from mine. "Forget it. It doesn't matter."

I let it go. He was right; it didn't matter. "You'll take care of us, I trust you."

Red snorted, tears in his voice. "Rule number one, Blue."

I frowned but decided it wasn't worth it to open that particular can of worms. Instead, I thought back to the fight at the warehouse.

"How did they find us?" I asked Red.

"I don't know," Red told me, his voice troubled. He carefully cleaned the head wound, wrapping fresh bandages around my head and helping me into the clean, dry scrubs. "I did a security sweep when we arrived. I had all my sensors monitoring the perimeter. The only way they could have known..." he trailed off.

"Is it if someone told them?" I finished for him, a hollow ache forming in my chest. "You don't think...?"

"If the Supes knew about the heist, they could have access to the Syndicate somehow," Red mused. "The Syndicate has a good working knowledge of most of the bunkers and safe houses local villains keep."

"A mole?" I suggested.

"Possibly," Red sighed. "We can't worry about it right now. We have to focus on finding somewhere safe. All my regular spots our out of the question, and I don't want to risk accessing any of my accounts if someone could be watching."

"I have a suggestion," Road Kill came through the door backwards, pulling a wheelchair. The wheels bumped rhythmically over the tile floor. "Found you a ride, Velvet!"

"Great," I said, eyeing the wheelchair dubiously.

"What's your suggestion, kid?" Red asked.

"There's an encampment I used to frequent out near the city limits. If we start now, we'd definitely make it there by daybreak. I'm tight with a bunch of people there; they'd be willing to take us in."

"You mean like a homeless encampment?" I asked.

"I know it's not the classiest solution, but it would definitely be the last place the Supes would look for us. Plus, there's one other major advantage." Road Kill paused for dramatic effect. "The Broker's people tend to pop in and out. It's the best place to try and get a meeting with them."

"I would have to be pretty damn desperate to want to go to the Broker for help," Red said, crossing his arms over his chest.

Road Kill spread his arms, gesturing to the bathroom. "This isn't desperate?" he asked.

"Sorry," I cut in. "Who's the Broker?"

Red turned to me, putting his back to Road Kill. "If there's anything close to the face of the Twilight Syndicate, it's the Broker. They know the ins and outs of the city's underworld and have access to resources that would make most villains' eyes water. But no one's ever seen them. They work through their contacts, and their help comes at a massive price."

"We have the Super Alliance's Mainframe." Road Kill pointed out.

"The Broker is dangerous," Red told him. "My priority is Velvet and the baby. I'm not risking them to chase a phantom."

"He's the only one who can help you." Road Kill said. "I saw your set up at the warehouse. It's going to be nearly impossible to find something like that in the wild. How else are you planning on hacking into the mainframe?"

Red was silent. Road Kill went on.

"Velvet doesn't have to be involved. I can put the word out that we have access to the Super Alliance's mainframe, and the Broker will come to us with an offer. Not to mention he'd be able to help us leak all the Super Alliance's dirty little secrets. We take them down, and they'll be too busy doing damage control to come after us."

"Or they swear revenge and we never know a moment's peace for the rest of our lives." Red countered.

"Or that," Road Kill agreed. "Either way, it's a place to rest and recover. Definitely, some people would be willing to put up *Blind Justice* over there. Especially in her delicate condition."

"My *condition*," I said tersely. "It is going to remain a secret. The Super Alliance doesn't need anything else to use against me."

"Absolutely," Road Kill agreed. "So, what do you think?"

Red shifted, uneasy. "I guess it's the best solution we have for now."

"Nice!" Road Kill jumped in triumph. "I'll let the others know. We should raid the medication. We'll need stuff to trade." He sprinted out the door.

"It's not ideal," Red mused.

"Better than nothing," I told him. "'Cause right now we have a whole lot of nothing."

"I have you." He was smiling big enough for me to see. It warmed me straight through.

"And I have you."

For now, it was enough.

Chapter Nineteen

The trek through the night left all of us half dead by the time the ragged shapes of the encampment came into view. Medea and Nefarious dragged behind, while Red stayed stubbornly at my side. In the dim morning light, I could only make out the silhouettes of broken tents and tarps. Smoke filled the air from barrel fires, thick with the stink of burnt plastic. The entire place reeked of sweat, diesel, and desperation.

Road Kill was behind me, guiding the wheelchair over the cracked asphalt. Each bump rattled through my side and the dull throb in my head. My hands fisted the thin blanket Red had tucked around me, as if I could disappear into the folds.

"This way," Road Kill said, his voice low. He knew the path by instinct, his boots crunching over familiar ground. "Don't trip over the pallets. Folks get territorial."

Heads lifted as we passed, and I could feel their gazes following us like a predator tracking wounded prey.

"Keep your heads down," Red muttered to us. His hand brushed the top of my shoulder before falling away. "Eye's forward, Blue."

"Eyes don't do me much good, Red." I hissed back.

A sharp bark of laughter from somewhere nearby made me flinch. Shapes stirred around the fire as we drew closer. Men and women, some clearly powered, with an iridescent glow around gloved hands, the flash of red eyes, the hum of electricity rising in the air.

"They know me," Road Kill assured us, forcing cheer into his tone. "It's cool."

The murmuring rose as we passed, whispering spreading like fire in dry brush. The shift in the crowd was obvious before we even reached the perimeter. Low voices rising. The stutter-pop of someone sparking their powers in warning.

"Sup, Guys!" Road Kill called out. "I brought some friends."

"Not a good time for new faces, Road Kill," a man barked. All I could see of him was his eyes, glowing faintly blue. "The Supes have raided us twice in the last three days. They took Melanie and David away for questioning, and you know they're not coming back."

"That's terrible," I whispered.

"We brought supplies, Anton," Road Kill told him. "Painkillers, antibiotics, vitamins. We even raided a few vending machines. Why don't we discuss over some Cheetos?"

"I told you—" Anton was cut off, some urgent whispers circling the group.

"Fuck," Anton murmured and sighed, resigned. "You brought antibiotics?"

"Several different strengths and varieties," Nefarious confirmed.

"Suzie's little one has a bad cough; we think it's an infection."

"Just point me in the right direction." Nefarious hoisted one of the supply bags over his shoulder.

"Hey, kids, take a look at this." Lights began to float and pop above the heads of the crowd. Several small forms broke off from the group to chase after them.

"Does that generator work?" Red asked. Anton grunted.

"Used to. Supers trashed it during the raid."

"Give me an hour or so, I'll have it up and running again," Red promised. "Just let me get my girl settled."

"I'm not leaving your side," I told him firmly, even while fighting to keep my eyes open.

"Road Kill will stay with you," Red assured me. "Let's just find you somewhere to lie down and rest."

Somewhere turned out to be a pile of old wooden pallets and a few thin blankets, but with how I was feeling, anything that wasn't the hard ground was acceptable.

Road Kill broke into the vending machine stash for me. I was ripping open the packages without bothering to see what they were, stuffing chips and cookies into my mouth faster than I could chew.

"Whoa," Road Kill said. "Slow down, Velvet."

He passed me a lukewarm bottle of water, and I gulped it down.

"Hey, Beth-Ann," Road Kill greeted. "Pringles?"

"Never say no to Pringles," Beth-Ann replied. She settled down next to us, smelling of hand sanitizer and mulch. "Wouldn't happen to have any Oxy? I haven't had a fix in weeks."

"Sorry," Road Kil said, and he sounded genuinely remorseful. "Nothing like that at the clinic we jacked. I do know I guy I could hit up in return for a favour."

"Road Kill," I hissed in disapproval.

"What favour?" Beth-Ann asked, ignoring me.

"I need you to put out some feelers," Road Kill explained. "We need to get a hold of the Broker."

"Road Kill!" I snapped in outrage and then froze, my stomach clenching painfully.

"I'm going to throw up," I said, panicked. Beth Ann and Road Kill jumped up, fumbling around us for a container. A too-small, plastic bucket was pushed into my hand just in time for me to vomit spectacularly into it.

"Fuck," I said when my stomach was finally empty. "Fuck, fuck, fuck."

"It's okay," Road Kill assured me. "I think there's some anti-nausea stuff in the bag."

The bag rustled, and I pushed away the container, which had begun leaking vomit onto my lap.

"Is she pregnant?" Beth Ann asked. "There are prenatal vitamins in the bag."

I nearly screamed in frustration, fumbling to snatch the bag out of Beth-Ann's hands.

"It's okay," she assured me, my swipes just out of reach. "I've had five of my own."

"I don't want it getting around," I insisted. "We shouldn't be talking about any of this!"

"Beth-Ann is good people," Road Kill assured me. "She's got connections."

"Rule number one, Road Kill," I bit out. "Forgive me if I don't want to spill all our secrets to a homeless Oxy addict."

I regretted it as soon as the words left my lips, but the damage was done.

"I won't take up any more of your precious oxygen than, *Blind Justice*," she sneered at me, getting to her feet. "Don't think you can just disappear here, the Supes are always watching."

"Beth-Ann, wait!" Road Kill called, but she was already storming off, passing Red and Medea as they returned.

"Not a good start if you're upsetting people already, Road Kill," Red said.

"Road Kill needs to learn to keep his mouth shut," I told them, irritated.

"What did you say?" Red demanded, his voice sharp.

Reluctantly, Road Kill recounted the conversation. Medea scoffed in disapproval.

"You shouldn't have mentioned the Broker," Red scolded. "Not without talking to me first."

"That's why we're here, isn't it?" Road Kill demanded. "To contact the Broker?"

"We're here," he said, settling down beside me. "To keep Velvet safe."

Road Kill took a moment to respond. It was light enough that I could make out the way he gestured theatrically around at the homeless encampment. "You call this safe? No one comes to a place like this to stay safe. Half the camp already knows she's here."

Red sighed, "I'm doing my best."

"And I'm trying to help." Road Kill told him pointedly. "She was pretty salty after Velvet snapped at her, but I promised to score her some Oxy if she put out the word."

Red didn't even hesitate. "No."

I sighed. "I don't like it either, but do we really have any other choice?"

"It's not a choice. It's making a deal with the devil."

"Red."

He cut me off with a hand on my shoulder, his grip tender but firm. "I said no. You don't trade the devil you know for the one hiding in the shadows. The Broker doesn't help people, Blue. He owns them."

"They're not wrong, though," Medea mused. "It's the only real lead we've had since we left the warehouse. Titan will not stop chasing us. We need leverage, and the Broker deals in leverage."

"Which makes him worse than Titan," Red snapped. "At least Titan doesn't pretend to be your friend first."

From behind us, Nefarious cleared his throat. I hadn't even realized he was nearby. "Medea has a point. A connection to the Broker, if genuine, cannot be ignored."

Red's voice was low and deadly, his hand on my shoulder squeezed ever so slightly. "We make our own choices. Not dance to some ghost's tune."

I sighed, wanting nothing more than to lie down and sleep for days. "Red, we can't keep running forever. Every day we're here is another day for the Supes to catch up. We need a plan."

Red's hands flexed restlessly. "And I'm telling you I won't sell our souls to some shadow whose only goal is to bleed us dry. Over my dead body."

"Fine," I agreed, exhaustion winning me over. "Let's just get some rest."

"You rest," he said. "I'll keep watch."

"Half dead, like you are?" Medea said. "I'd like to see that."

"If anyone comes calling, trust us, everyone will know." Road Kill assured us, even though it wasn't at all reassuring. "Get some sleep, man."

Red growled under his breath but relented, lying down next to me on the pallet. He was snoring in minutes.

I chuckled, settling down next to him and taking in his sleeping form, as much as I was able. The gentle huff of his breath was an excellent lullaby.

"You watch that one, Velvet," Medea told me, her voice soft. "He's liable to lose himself in all this."

I took a long breath, blowing it out slowly through pursed lips. "Sometimes I worry he already has."

Chapter Twenty

Five days into our stay at the camp found Red taking out his frustration on the camp's water filtration system. He'd been muttering under his breath for the better part of an hour before finally throwing down the rusted wrench in his hand.

"This thing has so many scavenged parts it's a miracle no one has been poisoned," he grumbled, dropping down next to me.

"They have to work with what they have," Medea told him.

"I know that," he snapped.

I put a hand on his leg, "Red," I said gently.

"Sorry," he muttered. "I'm sorry, Medea. This situation is completely out of my control, and I don't know what to do."

"It's okay," Medea assured him. "I don't blame you for being scared. Velvet picked a very inconvenient time to get pregnant."

"I'm not the only one to blame for that," I complained. My stomach lurched, and I reached for the bucket Nefarious had obtained for me to be sick in.

Red rubbed my back as I set the bucket aside; the scent of vomit seemed permanently fixed in my nose.

"It's getting worse." Red fretted.

"I'm fine," I insisted. "I can handle a little morning sickness."

"You're growing a person," Medea pointed out. "In very unusual circumstances. I agree with Cypher, this isn't sustainable."

There was a nearby shuffle, people whispering under their breaths.

"Shove off," Medea snapped. I heard a few shocked gasps and several pairs of feet running off.

"They're sizing us up," I guessed.

"People here know to distrust strangers," Medea confirmed. "We've come in with a reputation, it's enough to make anyone wary."

A sharp burst of static split the air, followed by a clipped voice barking orders. Red and blue lights painted the tents like flashing alarms, and the low hum of the camp turned to scattered panic.

Nefarious' ragged breaths preceded him as he rushed into the camp. "Fuck, I tried to go see Timmy, to make sure the new nanites were making progress, but his house is under surveillance. I don't understand. I didn't think they saw me."

"Shit," Red gasped. "Medea hide her. Nefarious with me."

Medea's hand was on my arm, tugging with firm pressure. I resisted.

"What are you going to do?" I demanded.

"We'll lead them away and scramble their radio signals." He assured me, "Meet back here when they're gone."

Medea pulled me to my feet. "Stay close, this way."

Her voice was calm as she guided me effortlessly through the sudden chaos, every step and instruction precise. Still, my injuries protested at the urgent pace.

"Ten more steps and we're going to duck behind a shelter," Medea told me. "We can stay there until they pass."

My legs felt like jelly, and my body screamed in protest as I leaned against the wall of the shelter, panting hard.

"Sorry," Medea whispered. "How bad is it?"

"I'm okay," I insisted, even as I sank to the ground and buried my head between my knees. I allowed the pain to wash over me, breathing deeply through the worst of it. Finally, when I'd recovered enough to speak, I lifted my head and focused on the place where I guessed Medea's eyes would be.

"Can I ask you something?"

She cocked her head. "Of course."

"When you got the job at the Miracle Network to keep an eye on me, were we really friends, or was that part of the act too?"

She stumbled over nothing, her shock palpable.

"What gave me away? She asked after a long, tense moment

"I'm blind, not stupid," I told her. "The more time I spend with Medea, the more Casey peeks through."

Medea sighed, "Casey is an act, but our friendship never was. I truly do care about you, Velvet."

I smiled, relieved despite myself. "I want you to be the baby's Godmother, you know."

"Yuck," Medea said. "No, thank you, I'll not be responsible for something that shits its pants regularly."

I laughed, "Red will be disappointed."

She snorted. "I highly doubt that."

A small commotion nearby was enough to distract us from our life-altering revelations. Raised voices carried over the rooftops. Medea helped me to my feet, and we followed the sound to the center of the encampment, a large fire lighting up the night.

"--I went to meet him about getting in contact with the Broker, and the Supes descended on the camp on twenty-fifth," Beth-Ann said in a rush. "I managed to get away, but the cops must have trailed me."

"Did they see you?" Anton demanded.

"No," Beth Ann said. "I don't think so."

"What contact?" I asked urgently, forgetting myself for a moment. "Would he have known what camp you were from?"

"Excuse me?" Beth Ann snarked, her voice cold.

I flushed, the atmosphere growing tense. I could feel the burn of the doubtful stares they cast upon me.

"It's a valid question," Medea insisted.

"Hazard wouldn't have said anything to the Supes." Anton insisted. "We look out for each other here."

"Hazard?" I gasped. "Hazard Waste?"

"Yes," Beth Ann confirmed, with deep reluctance. "I didn't say anything about you specifically, just that some people were looking for a meeting."

"So, this is what the slimeball has been doing since he ditched us." Medea huffed.

"How long has he worked for the Broker?" I asked.

"As long as I've known him," Beth Ann told us. "He's definitely no snitch, not that my word means much to you."

Medea sighed at her tone. "Alright, message received," she replied tersely and moved to lead me away.

Rule number one was on the tip of my tongue, but I bit it back.

When we informed the others, they didn't seem nearly as surprised as I had been. Still, as usual, Red couldn't hide his worry.

"We still don't know how the Supe's found the safehouse." He mused. "I don't like the idea of Hazard knowing where we are."

"Beth Ann said she didn't mention us," I told him.

"Doesn't mean he won't find out." Red sighed. "I guess for now, we wait."

Two weeks went by with five more raids on nearby homeless encampments. As they drew closer, Red became more anxious.

"We should leave." He said after another raid was reported only two blocks from us. Six people were arrested on unknown charges. "I can break into a computer store and try and transfer some funds from my offshore accounts."

"Not a good idea," Road Kill told him. "The Supes we'll be keeping tabs on shit like that. Here there are safety in numbers. If they raid, we can hide Velvet easier than if we're out in the open on our own."

"I'm right here," I told him irritably. I was having trouble keeping food down, and the lack of nutrition was leaving me lightheaded. "And it's not like I'm just going to hide while you guys get taken away."

"Medea and I already discussed what to do in case they come this way." Road Kill assured us. "She'll put up an illusion to hide us."

"Her illusions fail if someone comes in contact with them," Red pointed out. "By the sounds of it, when the Supers are finished, there isn't anything left standing."

"Well, I don't see you coming up with any bright ideas," Road Kill snarked.

I cut off their bickering by throwing up into the gutter.

When I finished, Red scooped me into his arms. It was the best move since my head was spinning and my ribs throbbed.

"I need to talk to Nefarious," Red grumbled. "You're vomiting a lot, constantly dehydrated. I'm worried."

"We're doing the best we can," I said, resting my head against his chest and closing my eyes. He carried me back to the tent we'd been staying in, laying me down in the corner and tucking the blankets around me even though the night was already too hot for comfort. My stomach was still raw, my ribs aching, but exhaustion dragged at me harder than the pain.

The interface in Red's armour dinged softly. "Someone left me a message," he mused, his visor lighting up.

"From the Broker?" I asked.

"No," Red said shortly. "Hazard."

The recording began to play, the audio choppy and slightly distorted. "Red, this is your last chance. The Broker won't wait forever, and neither will I. Titan wants the Oblivion formula, and they'll do anything to get it. Do what you want, but I'm out. I'm not going down for you." The recording cut off abruptly,

"What the hell does that mean?" I asked, baffled.

Shouting erupted from the far side of the encampment. Boots pounding, electricity crackling overhead. Someone screamed.

"Supes!" a voice roared. "They're here!"

I was hauled upright with brutal urgency, Red pulling me out into the night.

The ground shook beneath us as the first blast hit. A wall of heat and dust was rippling through the camp. People scattered like startled birds. Tents collapsed, flames licking through tarps and splintering wood.

Red dragged me against his side, half-carrying me as he pushed through the crush of bodies. I couldn't see the attackers, of course, only the flares of power cutting through the night. Blinding white arcs of lightning filled the sky, and bursts of fire roared like jet engines. The metallic tang of ozone flooded the air.

"Stay low," Red barked. His voice was a growl, tight and clipped. "Don't let go of me."

I clung to the chinks in his armour, the stench of burning plastic clawed at my throat. Somewhere ahead, Medea shouted, her voice high and sharp. The air bent around us, the screams muffled, the flames flickering oddly.

"Her illusion's up," Red called out. "Move, move!"

Nefarious appeared from the smoke, coughing hard. I could barely see him. He seemed to have something large slumped over his back, dragged along behind him. A groan confirmed it was Road Kill, though how badly he was hurt, I couldn't tell.

"They're coming from both ends!" Nefarious shouted. "We're boxed in!"

"We cut through," Red snapped back. His grip tightened on me, and I could feel the tremor of his heartbeat through his chest. "We don't stop, not for anything."

Behind us, the crash of metal reverberated as someone with super strength tore through a row of shacks like they were paper. The sound of it rattled inside my skull, too close, far too close.

"Left!" Medea's voice was sharp and insistent. The smoke curled oddly, forming a wall of darkness that seemed to swallow the world. Red didn't hesitate, dragging me straight through, the illusion bending to accommodate us.

Inside, everything was dulled. Sound, smell, even the heat. My senses muffled like cotton pressed against my face. I clung tighter to Red, fear buzzing in my chest.

"Just an illusion," I whispered, trying to reassure myself, but it was difficult. I'd never been a fan of the dark.

We plowed our way through the illusion until a beam of light split through the false-dark. My stomach lurched, disoriented.

"There!" A voice bellowed. "They're over there!"

Red cursed and scooped me into his arms. My stomach twisted at the sudden jolt. I clutched his neck, the world blurring around me.

Another blast slammed the ground nearby, a concussion that rattled my teeth.

"This way!" Road Kill roared, his voice raw. He barreled ahead, limping hard. "The south fence is weak, hurry!"

We reached the edge of camp. Red set me down long enough to shove me through a gap in the sagging chain-link fence, Medea pushing through right after. I scraped my hands on the wire, the bite of metal hot against my skin.

Then a flash, and the night turned white.

I turned my head instinctively, uselessly, but still felt the heat sear across my cheek. A Super, close, too close, shouted something I couldn't make out as power built in the air like a storm breaking.

Medea screamed, and Road Kill shouted something unintelligible.

And then Red was between us and the blaze, his body a shield. The impact never came, only silence.

The after flare blinded me completely, but sight wasn't necessary to know what happened as I listened to the buzz of Red's weapon powering down.

"Fuck, Cypher," Nefarious hissed. "Two dead Supers in less than a month."

"We need to keep moving," Red growled hoarsely. "Road Kill, can you stand?"

Road kill let out a pained grunt. "I'm good, let's go."

Behind us, the encampment burned. Sirens wailed, smoke billowed around us. The whole world felt like it was ready to collapse in on itself.

"I'm such an idiot´ Red said, hoisting me back into his arms. "Nowhere is safe."

I wanted to argue, to tell him we'd find somewhere else, anywhere else, but the words stuck in my throat.

All I could do was clutch my stomach and feel the faint flutters I wasn't sure were real, and wonder if we'd be running forever.

Chapter Twenty-One

We ended up climbing down into a sewer with a loose cover. As soon as my feet touched ground, the smell had me doubling over, dry heaving violently over the disgusting floor.

Medea was at my side, her broken illusion still flickering around the edges of her body and making my stomach roll.

"I have some anti-nausea remedies," Nefarious said, rooting through his bag. He was still coughing, the sound rattling through his frame.

"Any water?" Red asked, coming to kneel at my side, his hand on my face as I tried to steady myself. "She's very dehydrated."

"That's a no on the water," Nefarious said.

"What?" Red strolled over and took the bag, the contents shifting furiously as he rooted through it. "You have three different spools of wire in here, but didn't think to grab some water? Or food for that matter?"

"Everything was on fire," Nefarious protested. "It wasn't on my mind to pack for a long trip."

Pounding footsteps came from above, police sirens screaming through the streets.

"So, we have no food, no water and nowhere to go?" Road Kill surmised. "That's great."

"What about an illusion?" I suggested, head spinning. I dropped down onto the damp floor, my clothes instantly soaking through. "Just to get us somewhere safe."

"I don't know what that Supe hit me with, but my powers aren't working right," Medea admitted. "I'm going to need time to get them back under control."

"Velvet?" Red asked, his voice sounded strange, like he was calling to me through a tunnel. "Velvet, can you hear me?"

Suddenly, I was flat on my back with the others circling me.

"Wha...?" I began. Nefarious took my wrist, checking my pulse. I was covered in a cold sweat, and my mouth tasted like bile. The dark closed in, clouding my limited vision. I reached up blindly, and Red grasped my hand tightly.

"Pulse erratic, fever climbing. It could be placental abruption, could be infection. Velvet swallow." A tablet was placed on my tongue, and I managed to force it down my throat. "She needs a sterile environment and proper monitoring. I can't do anything with scavenged tubing and wishful thinking."

"I don't know if you noticed, doc, but we're limited on options right now," Road Kill pointed out.

"There must be something you can do," Red practically begged, his voice breaking like glass.

"I'm sorry, Cypher," Nefarious said, sounding like he deeply meant it. "My hands are tied without the right equipment."

The words hung in the air like a death sentence. I could feel Red's eyes on me as he pressed my hand to his chest. His heart pounded like a hammer under my palm.

"Fuck," he whispered. His suit buzzed to life, the interface on his gauntlet glowing in the dim light.

"What are you doing?" Medea asked.

"Contacting the Broker," he told us.

"What?" Medea demanded, her voice echoing down the tunnel.

"How?" Nefarious gasped.

"They contacted me three days ago. I told them to go fuck themselves."

I pressed my eyes closed, swallowing hard. "You should have told us." I had to force the words out, each one a massive effort.

"I didn't want us indebted to that prick," Red rushed out. "I didn't want to put our lives in the hands of a fucking ghost."

"And now?" Medea demanded.

"Oh, like I have a fucking choice?" Red snapped. "With the woman I love half dead on a sewer floor?"

A persistent beeping came through the communication system in Red's suit, then the click of a call connecting.

"Mr. Cypher," a smooth robotic voice intoned. "I'm surprised to be hearing from you again. Especially, after our last conversation."

"I'm willing to prove to you the Dead Channel exists in the Titan mainframe."

"Really? How excellent. I must admit I was beginning to think this was all some form of complicated hoax. A ploy to get my attention."

"It's very real," Red assured him. "I'm willing to do whatever you want, but we've got wounded and we need medical help."

There was a long, heavy pause.

"Would I be right in guessing Ms. Walker requires assistance?" The Broker guessed. "She is in a delicate condition, after all."

The words were like an axe held over our heads. I could practically hear Red grinding his teeth. "We need help." Was his only answer.

"Very well," The Broker said, casually as though making lunch plans. "In five minutes, the street will clear of police. You'll have a two-minute window to get to the black sedan parked at the end of the road. It will take you somewhere safe."

"So, what, you control the cops now?" Road Kill blurted.

"I have many connections, Mr. Wade." The Broker said.

"We're just supposed to get into a random car that will drive us to a mystery location?" Red said, understandably skeptical.

"You have a total of seven minutes before the car leaves, with or without you in it." The Broker warned. "What you decide is no consequence to me. Make your choice."

The call ended.

Red was the first to move, gathering me up in his arms and moving towards the ladder.

"The rest of you need to get as far away from here as possible," Red told the others. "Wait until morning if you have to and flee the city. You should be able to—"

"Okay, shut up." Medea interrupted, coming to his side. "I'll go first, and you pass her up to me, and we'll head for the car. You idiots coming?"

I could hear the shuffle as Nefarious gathered up his pack.

"I can go first and get the cover," Road Kill suggested. "Do you want me to carry your pack, Doc?

Red was shaking his head in disbelief. "I can't ask you to—"

"Already told you to shut up," Medea repeated. "Go ahead, Road Kill, I'll get the bag."

Together, they managed to haul me up the ladder like a sack of potatoes. I kept fading in and out of consciousness, the awkward movements jarring old injuries and making my nausea worse. I blinked and found myself lying on the back seat of a spacious vehicle, the windows tinted and the seat smelling of leather. A bottle of water was pressed to my lips, and I drank greedily, gulping down large mouthfuls until the bottle was pulled away.

"There's some food here," Road Kill said.

"Don't give her anything while she's half-conscious," Nefarious warned. "She'll choke."

My stomach disagreed, but I was in no shape to give an opinion.

"Red," I murmured.

"Right here, Blue." He took my hand, the other running over my hair. "You're going to be just fine."

"The baby," I pressed.

"The little demon is strong, Velvet," Medea told me. "Don't worry."

The only noise was the smooth hum of tires over cracked asphalt and the occasional rattle as the car bottomed out. Every bump shot pain through me, but the silence seemed too heavy to break.

No one spoke, no one dared. We were in the lair of the beast. Anyone could be listening.

When the car finally slowed, the others leaned forward as if pulled by the same invisible string. The engine cut. Doors unlocked with a soft click.

We exited into a private garage lined with polished concrete, the kind that echoes too loudly under your shoes. An elevator waited with its doors already opened, humming low and inviting.

Red cradled me close as it carried us up. I was sweating under the collar of my shirt. My palms pressed to my stomach like I could shield the little life residing there.

"Holy shit," Road Kill whistled as we entered. "It's like one of those showrooms from a magazine."

"Look at this bathroom!" Medea exclaimed. "I've lived in houses smaller than this."

"Cypher, there's a bedroom in here. Bring Velvet." Red followed the sound of Nefarious' voice into a wide bedroom with white sheets, folded blankets, and soft pillows. I could hear Nefarious rummaging through cabinets, pulling out medical supplies.

"Fucking hell," Red whispered, setting me down on the soft bed.

"What?" I asked, trying to follow the line of his sight but only managing to make my head spin.

Red swallowed. "There's a bassinet and a bunch of baby stuff."

"Shit," I whispered.

"News certainly gets around," Nefarious said, wrapping a blood pressure cuff around my arm and lifting my shirt to run a probe over the soft curve of my stomach. The faint static whine filled the room before it broke into the fast, rabbit-quick thrum of a heartbeat. My throat tightened, tears prickling the corners of my eyes.

"He's steady," Nefarious assured us. "Heartbeat within range, lungs clear. No uterine bleeding I can detect. Whoever stocked this place had access to premium obstetric supplies. Makes my job easier at least."

Red moved towards the cabinets, pulling out a can of what I thought might be baby formula. "They're planning for us to be here a while."

"Don't let them get in your head," Nefarious warned, smoothly pushing a needle into my arm and hanging an IV to start a drip.

"What's that?" I asked because I thought I ought to. Exhaustion was crushing me flat.

"Saline and antibiotics," Nefarious explained. "Just a precaution, I think you're mostly just malnourished and dehydrated, but I'm going to monitor for sepsis."

I nodded, letting my eyes fall shut.

Red sat down next to me, the bed sinking under his weight. He reached out and rested a hand on my stomach, the warmth of his palm flowing through me.

"Tell me I did the right thing." He whispered,

"We didn't have a choice," I slurred, sleepily.

He heaved a hard breath. "I've never made the best decisions backed into a corner."

Chapter Twenty-Two

It was a while before the Broker contacted us again.

Red tried to get in contact, but the channel they had used remained firmly closed. It made him angry and irritable. The atmosphere became hostile and tense. On the third day, I put my foot down as much as I was able.

I healed fast with access to proper food and medical supplies. Nefarious was pleased with my progress, and Medea had been helping me map out the penthouse, so I was able to find my way around easily. A brand-new white cane had been provided for my use. Like everything else in the penthouse, its presence felt like a sword dangling over our heads.

"Three more steps to the kitchen island," Medea told me. "Five steps to the right to the end and then five steps forward to reach Cypher, who is brooding."

Red slammed the cabinet door. The sound cracked like a gunshot in the stillness.

"He's keeping us locked in this gilded cage like animals. I knew this was a bad idea."

"Maybe that's the point," Medea said as she guided me to sit on the Island, the stool high enough that my feet dangled like a child. "Keeping you simmering until you boil over."

"Shut up," Red snapped. His voice held an edge that made everyone freeze. Even Nefarious, who usually loved to poke the bear, said nothing.

"Red," I admonished.

He ignored me, pacing the length of the kitchen, my eyes tracking the red blur of his uniform. Every heavy step shook the glassware. "We're just sitting here, waiting to be played. That's all this is. A goddam joke. Hazard was right, we're not even hiding anymore, we're pets."

"Hazard is a lying sack of dicks," Medea reminded him. "I'd expect you to be above the word of that traitor."

"I'd expect you to mind your own fucking business." Red snarled.

"Red!" My voice sharpened, cutting through the room. He stopped, his form so tight and still, he was liable to snap. I held out my hand to him, "Please."

He sighed and crossed to me, taking my offered hand, sitting down next to me and hanging his head. "You're making it worse." I told him softly but unflinching." Not for the Broker, he doesn't give a fuck. The only people you're hurting are us. Me."

His hand twitched, but he didn't pull away. I guided his palm to my stomach, where the baby shifted faintly beneath my ribs. "You feel that?"

He swallowed hard, jaw locked.

"We're not waiting for the Broker. We're waiting because we don't have a choice. You raging around doesn't change that; it just makes everyone more afraid, including me."

The silence stretched, heavy. Finally, I felt his shoulders slump, some of the fight bleeding out of him. "We shouldn't have needed him in the first place. I should be able to take care of you, both of you, without relying on some faceless asshole."

"You are taking care of us," I promised him. "We are doing what we have to, to stay safe. As long as we're breathing, we still have choices. Don't make the wrong one out of anger."

His head bowed, forehead brushing mine for a fleeting moment before he pulled away.

"I'll try."

I smiled, "That's all I'm asking."

"You two are adorable," Medea crooned.

"Shut up," Red sighed, the words lacking the bite they held before.

It became easier then, if not less stressful, waiting around for something, anything to happen. The news didn't report any of the raids on homeless encampments, or even anything about our escape. However, two weeks into our stay a special broadcast had us all reeling.

"My name is Lisa Monore. My son Timothy Monore was diagnosed with an inoperable brain tumour last year."

Nefarious let out a low gasp. "Oh no, Timmy," he whispered.

"We had lost all hope until Doctor Nefarious came to us with an unlicensed procedure using tiny robots to shrink the tumour. He didn't ask for money. He didn't make promises he couldn't keep. He said he had the technology to help, and he did. I watched the scans myself. The tumour was shrinking. My son started smiling again. He said he wanted to go outside and ride his bike. For the first time in months he wasn't in pain.

"The procedures stopped when the Super Alliance began staking out our house, making it impossible for Doctor Nefarious to continue. Without him, the tumour came back and within three weeks, Timmy was gone.

She paused, quiet sobs echoing through the microphone.

"For a brief few moments, my husband and I had our son back. We had hope where there had been none before. As far as I'm concerned, the Super Alliance is the reason my son is dead. There is no doubt in my mind that Doctor Nefarious would have cured him if he'd been permitted to continue the treatments.

"My son's death calls into question everything we've been told about Velvet

Walker and the villains she was working with. I will never be able to put my trust in the Super Alliance ever again, and I implore everyone watching to think critically about the Super Alliance and Titan Global's motives going forward.

"If helping my son makes a man a criminal, then maybe the real villains are the ones who stopped him."

The broadcast ended. We were left in a heavy silence.

Nefarious stood and walked to his room without a word.

"The Super Alliance is going to pay for all the pain they've caused," Red promised.

"If only you'd been able to access the Dead Channel," Medea lamented. "We could have exposed them with every piece of dirt stuck in the mainframe."

"We still can," I said, earnestly from my place tucked into Red's side, cuddled in the corner of the couch. "I mean, the Broker's going to want a return on his investment eventually."

I felt Red clench his jaw, his body tensing against me. "If he hasn't forgotten about us." He grumbled.

A familiar face appeared on the screen.

"Known supervillain Hazard Waste was arrested today, after a six-hour standoff with police and members of the Super Alliance. He is being held without bail in the city penitentiary..."

"Well, isn't that just too bad?" Road Kill chuckled.

Medea sighed in pleasure. "Ah, karma."

"That doesn't make sense," Red mused. "I thought he was under the Broker's protection. That was the reason he sold us out, wasn't it?"

A speaker crackled overhead, making all of us start. "You will find me to be a fickle mistress, Red Cypher."

"Fucking hell!" Medea squawked and Road Kill stood straight up in alarm.

"Apologies," The Broker's voice said. "I didn't mean to impose, but I'm afraid the time has come for Mr. Cypher to fulfill his end of our bargain."

Red gently detangled himself from me, standing slowly. "I was ready the minute we arrived. You're the one who's been taking their sweet time."

The Broker didn't reply. Instead, there was a sound from Red's suit like a file being uploaded. The built-in computer chimed expectantly.

"I've given you access to a sealed connection, quarantined from every network but the one you've already breached. Safe, invisible. The perfect vessel for your backdoor."

Red took a steadying breath. "Alright, so what do you want me to do?"

"I have uploaded a document which details which files I would like you to download from the mainframe. Do this without triggering their security, and I will be willing to discuss future enterprises. Fail and I'm afraid you're extended vacation will come to an end."

"He says it like it's an actual threat," Red murmured as he sat back down. I focused closely on his movements as he pressed a hand against his chest, a keyboard sliding out from a secret compartment. The television screen went momentarily dark before flickering back to life, now filled with symbols and colours I couldn't make out.

Red ran his fingers over the keyboard, like a concert pianist, preparing to play a symphony.

His fingers flew over the keyboard so quickly that it hummed. The flashing lights on the TV filled the room.

"Alright," Red murmured as he worked. "First up, operation expenditure logs."

The clicking of the keyboard was almost musical as Red read out each file. With each one he pulled from the ether, his voice became more animated, clearly in his element.

"Hero licensing database, easy, barely any security. Incident suppression reports, going to save that one for later. Containment protocols, active facilities only, might as well pull all of them while I'm here."

The others watched, captivated, and I was momentarily envious of their ability to take in all the details of what was happening.

"Communication index, encrypted transmissions, that's a bit trickier."

Nefarious reappeared from his room to watch the spectacle. "Now you're just showing off."

"Just watch the master work," I could hear the grin in Red's voice, and then suddenly the sound of the keyboard cut off, the screen went still.

"Red?" I asked, confused.

"Oh shit," Medea said, leaning towards the television. Road Kill gave a low whistle.

My heart leaped into my throat. "Someone tell me what's going on!" I demanded.

"The last two files," Red said. "Personal and medical records of Morag and Velvet Walker and Oblivion Research Case files, Project Walker 01 and 02."

"Oblivion?" Nefarious balked. "What does Velvet have to do with Oblivion?"

"You told me it had been off the streets for years." Road Kill said.

"That's why he killed her," the horrid realization washed over me like ice water.

"What are you talking about, Blue?" Red asked. The entire room had gone quiet enough to hear a pin drop.

"Black Bullet killed my mother," I confessed. "I figured it out the night of the ball after he left a hair on my dress. The DNA matched what I found on my mother the night she died. He wanted Oblivion, and she refused to give it to him."

"I don't understand," Nefarious asked. "How did you know it was the same DNA?"

"Later," Red told him, his fingers flying over the keyboard. In a matter of seconds, Red had finished pulling the remaining files, the computer's hum winding down as he closed the Dead Channel and sat back in his seat.

"Well done, Mr. Cypher." The Broker intoned over the speaker system.

"Son of a bitch," Road Kill muttered. "I wish they'd stop doing that!"

"You wanted us to see that," Red surmised.

"I need you to study those particular files in preparation for your next task." The Broker told us.

"Next task?" Red snapped. "You said you wanted me to prove the Dead Channel existed. I proved it!"

"That was to ensure you are trustworthy." The Broker explained with the cadence of someone talking to a small child. "Now, if you wish for my further assistance, then I need something in return, something more substantial than a locked door only you can open."

"What then?" I demanded, anger blossoming in my cheeks.

"You've already stumbled upon the logical conclusion," The Broker told us. "I want the formula for Oblivion."

"So, I've heard," Red said.

"How the hell are we supposed to get that?" Medea asked, incredulous. "No one knows who supplied it. It disappeared from the streets."

"I would suggest consulting your mother, Ms. Walker." The Broker said. "You have one month." The speaker cut out with a sharp click, the silence sudden and heavy.

I sat utterly frozen, barely able to breathe through the shock of it.

"Hold the fuck on," Road Kill barked, his fist slamming against the wall. "You told me that shit was gone, Velvet!"

His anger hit like fire against my skin.

"I..." My mouth had gone dry. "It was. It is!"

"Bullshit!" His voice cracked with desperation. "How could you not have known? It's out there, but I'm stuck here suffering with this curse!"

"I swear, I didn't know!" I insisted.

Nefarious was pacing behind us, his bare feet slipping over the carpet. "Oblivion was a whisper when I was still in grad school. A classified pharmacological experiment. Half urban legend, half horror story. But a working formula? That's impossible, it doesn't exist."

"Apparently it does!" Road Kill huffed

"Let's not put the cart before the horse, Road Kill. It was a very unstable substance, related to many overdoses." Nefarious explained. "Supplies started running out around two years ago; it was about a year before that when the supplier disappeared."

"Around the same time, I passed the bar exam." I sank into the couch, my hands searching for the blanket I'd left there.

"A little farther to your left," Medea advised. I found the blanket and wrapped it around my shoulders.

"My mom never talked about it, but I knew she was selling drugs on the side," I admitted, the words slipping out before I could stop them, bitter and quiet. "There was no other way she could've afforded law school or the house, or anything after the university fired her."

Road Kill shifted, the floor squeaking under his feet. "So, what? We just dig her up and ask her?"

"That's not funny," I snapped.

Red sighed and came to sit down next to me, a reassuring hand on my shoulder. "Maybe a little more tact, next time, Road Kill, but you're not wrong. She's the only person who would have answers, and she's rotting in the ground."

Nefarious stopped pacing. "There have to be files, documentation. If she created Oblivion, she would've left records, notes, experiments, something. A scientist's research doesn't just disappear."

"There wouldn't be anything about it at the university," I mused. "She brought all her work home with her. But the Super Alliance would have descended on the house as soon as they got the warrant to arrest me. Anything of use would have been seized."

"But there was nothing about the formula in the mainframe." Red pointed out. "The only files mentioning it were the ones I pulled, and if they said anything about the formula, the Broker wouldn't have ordered us to find it."

"Could your mother have hidden the files somewhere in the house, Velvet?" Medea asked. "Perhaps somewhere only you'd know to look."

"I have no idea," I admitted. "But even if she did, the house has to be under surveillance. How would we even get in?"

Medea scoffed, "Oh, please, child's play."

"Not quite," Red countered. "We'd have to plan it out carefully. Do some reconnaissance. It'll take time."

My stomach twisted. "And if we get in and there's nothing?"

Red sighed. "It's the only lead we've got."

Chapter Twenty-Three

Over the next week, the others took turns circling the neighbourhood where I grew up. Not too close, never too close, but just near enough to watch the rhythms of the house that no longer belonged to me.

Medea's illusions made them shadows on the street corners, ghosts in parked cars and sometimes even part of the scenery itself. Road Kill had a knack for blending into alleys and rooftops, scaling places that would have been impossible for anyone else. Nefarious spent his time sketching maps on the high-quality note paper, which seemed to be in endless supply at the penthouse, plotting entry points and camera blind spots with the precision of a man wiring a bomb.

"It's not just a house anymore," Red told me after he and Medea returned from yet another stakeout of the property. "Titan's got it flagged as an active crime scene. That means reinforced locks, sensors tied to the main grid and most likely a hidden failsafe. If we go in, we do it fast. One misstep and they'll bury it under a task force before we get out."

"Cheery," Medea said, throwing herself down on the couch beside me, making the cushions bounce. "We break in, we break out. Easy as breathing."

"Easy for you to say," Road Kill cut in. "You turned yourself into a fire hydrant when the police got too close."

"It's not my fault, I am perfect." She countered.

Their bickering faded into the background as I leaned back into the couch and continued the audio file I'd been listening to on the tablet Red had set up for me. A computerized voice read the files commandeered from the Titan's mainframe in a calm monotone.

"Subject: Morag Walker. Research designation: Project Oblivion. Primary outcome Neurochemical destabilizer with high dependency yield..."

The words stripped her bare, turned her into a case number, a cog in their machine.

"...strain three-seven-six demonstrates increased viability, recommend further trials for scaled distribution..."

I should've stopped. Instead, I leaned closer, heart in my throat, until the voice reached the line that made the room tilt around me.

"V. Walker had shown no signs of superhuman abilities despite the abilities of Morag Walker and REDACTED. However, in the case of hereditary pass-through, subject V. Walker's offspring may provide a viable sequence for genetic acquisition. Samples recommended in the third trimester..."

I pressed a hand against my stomach, bile rising at every word. My mother's name woven into something monstrous, my child treated like a science experiment.

I didn't even notice Red move until his hand closed over mine, silencing the tablet. "That's enough for today, Blue."

"They know who my father is," I told him as he settled in beside me. "His name has been taken out of every file, but they know."

"Yes, I noticed too," Red agreed. "There are several instances of it throughout the documents. One very clear thing is that Titan arranged her death. You need to read between the lines, but it's obvious when you know what to look for."

"Black Bullet killed her," I corrected. "He must have really wanted that formula if he was willing to get his hands dirty. I can't wait to see his face when we burn his world down."

Red sighed and pulled me gently onto his lap, cradling me close, one hand on the curve of my belly.

"We don't have to do this, you know," he said. "I have access to my accounts now. I could book us tickets on the next flight to Morocco if you wanted. We could leave this all behind."

It was hard not to consider it, trapped in our own personal surveillance state, with a host of vengeful gods breathing down our necks.

"We can't," I told him, hugging the tablet to my chest. "I can't. I have to know the truth. Black Bullet killed my mother over this. I can't let him get his hands on it. Not after everything we've been through.

Red didn't argue. He shifted slightly, sliding something small and smooth into my hand. A key drive, but unlike any I'd encountered before.

"You need to plug this directly into your tablet. It is the key to the Dead Channel. With this, you can access the back door anywhere. It'll stay dormant until you enter the access code."

He took my fingers, guiding them over the tablet's screen in a very distinct pattern. He made my fingers go through the pattern three more times and then twice on my own to make sure I'd memorized it. "When you run it, it will tunnel through Titan's defences and land you inside the system. Every file, every document, every secret. I'm working on a program that will disperse any files we select to the major news hubs and social media sites, but it's not done yet."

"Once we do that, they'll start to pull all the incriminating stuff from the mainframe." I pointed out. "We'd only get one shot."

"I'm still ironing out the logistics," Red admitted. "It's still dangerous for them, leverage for us."

My fingers hovered over the tablet, trembling. "Why are you trusting me with this?

"Because trust is all I've got left," he said simply. His hand came to rest over mine, steadying it against the screen. "If something happens to me, you'll still have the key. It'll keep you safe."

I leaned back against him, exhaling slowly, pressing the words into my memory. "What happened to rule number one?"

He gave a low laugh against my ear and settled his arms around me. "I remembered rule number two. Never forget what we're fighting for."

Chapter Twenty-Four

The house loomed like a distant ghost. I could still map the floor plan in my mind. Each creaking stair, every loose floorboard and lifting carpet. However, the way it felt now was different. It wasn't my home anymore; it was a tomb.

The grass outside had grown wild, the ends brushing my ankles as I leaned against the chain-link fence Titan had, half-heartedly, wrapped around the yard. Motion sensors buzzed nearby, a sterile rhythm like the beat of a mechanical heart.

"Side door's clear," Road Kill whispered, crouched low. "Camera loop holding."

"Keep your voices down," Red growled, his hand closing over mine. His heat and weight grounded me as he guided me forward, step by step, across the broken path. My new cane tapped lightly against the cracked stone walkway, but his grip shifted each time, steering me clear of obstacles.

I smelled mildew and rotten leaves. My throat tightened. I'd grown up here. Now every corner reeked of abandonment.

We'd gone over the plan too many times to count. Red's signal blocker would only hold for half an hour tops. The camera loop would stay undetectable indefinitely, or until someone on the other end noticed. It would be up to me to lead them to any possible places where my mother might have hidden sensitive material. If anything went wrong, the plan was to smuggle me out the back while Red and Medea created cover. I chose to ignore that last part.

Medea crouched by the door, whispering a few syllables under her breath. A shimmer passed across the frame, and for a second it almost sounded like laughter, but then the lock clicked open, smooth as silk.

"Welcome home," she teased.

I swallowed hard and stepped inside.

The air was stale, the way a room feels when it's been shut too long. I smelled dust, dry wood and underneath it, something faintly chemical. Not enough to name, just enough to make my skin crawl.

"Lights are tripped," Nefarious muttered. "They rigged this place as bait."

Red's hand squeezed mine. "Then we don't linger."

The others fanned out, Road Kill scouting ahead, a knife glinting in his hand. Medea trailed illusions along the windows to blur our presence. Nefarious muttered to himself about circuits and charge.

I immediately headed for the study, my feet easily finding the familiar path. The air still held the barest essence of my mother, herbal tea and essential oils.

Red stayed close to me, his arm a constant tether. "Talk to me, Blue. What are you feeling?"

Anger, grief, longing. My whole being yearned for my mother. I sighed and brushed my fingertips along the wall, the paint flaking under my nails. "I can feel all the time she spent here, hours bent over research and chemical compounds." My senses prickled, my skin alive with faint traces. "There's residue. Ink, chemicals, something metallic. If she left something behind, it would be here."

"Okay," Red said. "I want to say take your time, but..."

"I know," I told him, taking a few tentative steps further in. The desk was still there, for the first time, clear of books and notes. My fingers traced over the scratches and dings built up over the years. I tapped my cane over the floor, trying my best to walk in a grid so as not to miss anything.

I made it to the far wall. My fingers ghosted over the wood panels. I knocked on the wall, listening for any hollow spaces. Knock, step, knock, step. I began to feel discouraged. Had this all been for nothing?

Then something sparked against my other sense. Strange and unexpected.

"This is laminate." I realized. My brain was reading the molecular contrast like a book. "The rest of the panels are hardwood, but this one is laminate."

"It looks identical," Red said, coming to stand at my side.

I ran my fingers over the edges, nails digging into the seams.

"Here," Red said. He pulled something from the wall, a carved detail, and the panel fell off the wall with a thud. I reached out, and my hands found the door to a vault, my palms pressed to the cool metal. My ability flared sharply. Compounds bloomed in my mind. Steel, grease, faint traces of plastic polymers from the dial. And barely there, chemical signatures I'd touched before but never had a name for. Now I knew what it had to be, what it had always been. Oblivion.

"Hey! Velvet found something!" Road Kill called from the door. Footsteps raced towards the study, the others crowding close. However, my whole world had narrowed to the vault's dial, the faint hum of danger in the walls and the sick twist in my stomach.

I lowered my ear to the door, the dial cool and rough under my fingertips, each ridge distinct like the spine of a predator.

"There are no numbers on the dial," Nefarious observed.

"She's got this," Red warned the others, voice tight.

"What's she going to do?" Medea scoffed. "Hug it open?"

"Shh," I hissed, and their voices immediately fell away.

I took a steadying breath, rolling the dial carefully under my touch. The tumblers clicked, faint, almost inaudible, but to me, each shift carried weight. The smallest vibration resonates through my skin. And beneath those mechanics, there was something else. The faint ghost of compounds used in oiling the gears, the resin of her gloves where she touched it last. My mother's fingerprints in chemical form.

"I can feel it," I hushed, my breath creating condensation on the metal. "She really didn't want this found."

The first tumbler fell with a satisfying *click*. A rush of adrenaline hit me like I'd broken the first seal on a coffin.

I turned again, slower, hunting for the next break. The metal hummed in my palm, compounds shifting. Iron, nickel, graphite, grease. Then another catch. Another *click*.

"Holy shit," Road Kill whispered.

"Shh," Medea warned.

I exhaled through my nose, steadying my hands. My ribs ached with the pressure of leaning forward. The last tumbler was faint, almost lost in the whisper of friction. My fingers burned with sensitivity, every trace compound sparking like fire through my nerves.

"Come on, Mom," I murmured under my breath. "Let me in."

The dial shuddered. Then, *click*.

The latch released.

I stumbled back as the heavy door swung open. It was dark inside, making it impossible for me to see what we'd uncovered.

"Notebooks," Red said, pulling them out of the safe. "She took the time to waterproof everything. Thumb drives, one of them has your name on it, Velvet. And—holy shit---"

"What is it?" I asked, but I could smell it as Red pulled a slim glass vial from the vault and handed it to me.

"Oblivion," I said, without a doubt in my mind. The compound signature screamed against my senses. Sharp, wrong and acidic in a way that made my teeth ache.

"That vial holds the type of power that gets people killed," Nefarious said.

"Road Kill," I said. "Take it."

Road kill hesitated. "Seriously?" Red held it out to him, the glass clinking as it changed hands.

"Alright, let's grab what we can and get out of here," Red ordered.

"Take everything," I insisted. "If we leave it here, it'll just fall into the wrong hands."

"She's right," Nefarious agreed. There was a shuffle as they hurried to pack up the vault's contents.

"She kept this for you," Medea told me. "She knew one day that someone would come after you for it."

"She should have just told me," I muttered bitterly.

"And what would you have done?" Medea asked. "Told her to turn herself in?"

"No!" I gasped, "Of course not."

Medea made an unconvincing noise. "Either way, she was protecting you. Your ignorance is what's kept you alive this long."

"Wise woman, your mother." Black Bullet mused from the study door.

He'd managed to bypass the proximity alarm we set up and Medea's illusions. Road Kill cursed in shock, Red and Medea automatically moved to shield me, while Nefarious fumbled the items in his hands, the lot of it clattering to the floor.

Black Bullet stepped into the study, his presence sucking the air from the room. The gleam of his armour marked his movement, every step deliberate, like a man who'd already won.

Red's suit buzzed, weapons charging. The air shimmered at Medea's fingertips, and I heard the distinct *shink* of Road Kill's knife as he pulled it from its case. Every one of them was tensed, ready to strike.

But Black Bullet didn't rush. He strolled forward, each step punctuated by the echoing click of his boots. "You've all done well. Survived longer than anyone expected. For sewer rats, you're clever, resourceful, but it's over now. You've lost."

"Go fuck yourself," Red snarled.

"No need to be rude," Black Bullet went on. "I am a reasonable man, and you all have a lot to offer. Titan is willing to be very generous if any of you wanted to switch sides."

"Oh, you can fuck all the way off with that shit," Road Kill told him, furious.

"Are you sure, Road Kill?" Black Bullet said, his voice laced with false concern. "How many nights have you woken up wishing you could just be like everyone else? The thought of all the people around you growing old and dying while you just keep regrowing limbs and organs over and over. How long before it drives you mad? Oblivion could take it all away."

"You offer what we've already given him," Medea warned. "We won't fall for false promises."

"Even if I offer the person who betrayed your parents?" Black Bullet asked, and I felt her go unnaturally still. "I know the name of their killer, Medea. I can have him delivered to you."

"And, of course, the good doctor." Black Bullet continued, calm and collected, like he had all the time in the world. "So noble of you to help those innocent children. Your expertise could have saved several lives. Timmy was a tragedy. I could help ensure it never happens again. Reinstate your medical license so you can work above board. Think of all the lives you could save. Clear some of that red from your ledger."

Nefarious swallowed hard but said nothing.

"It wouldn't be too far a leap, you know. Considering I'm the one who's been keeping you alive all this time. Filling your cupboards supplied you with food, medicine, and a comfortable bed."

"No fucking way," I muttered.

"I'm afraid so," Black Bullet's voice was almost giddy. "I am the Broker. Hazard Waste was my loyal minion until he found out. He almost succeeded in warning you, but I was able to alter the message."

"Fuck," Red breathed. "I fucking should've known. My gut told me there was something off."

"And what would you have done?" Black Bullet sneered. "Run back to the sewer and watch your child die just like you did with Samuel? He never did bother to tell you the truth, did he, Velvet? That Red Cypher is your old friend, Aiden Hall. The father who couldn't even look at you at his son's funeral."

"He didn't need to tell me," I blurted out, determined to wrestle back a modicum of control. "I knew. I've known for a long time. I was waiting for him to tell me on his terms."

Red's eyes were on me. His gaze was like a beacon, giving me strength as I plowed onward. "You think you can divide us? Promise us the moon and the stars, and we'll just roll over? Fuck you. Rule number one: never trust a villain!"

Black Bullet's voice turned low and cold. "I am no villain. I am your father; that baby you're carrying is my grandchild. You have no idea the kind of power it could have. I can protect you, both of you. Your mother always hoped we'd reconcile. Did you know she named you after one of her favourite songs? *Black Velvet.*"

I laughed. I couldn't help it. His entire bullshit speech was a perfect example of everything I hated about this man.

"The song was *Blue Velvet*," I spat. "Don't pretend to know me. You labelled me as damaged goods the moment I was born. You killed my mother when she was no longer of any use to you. You don't get to come back and demand things now."

Black Bullet chuckled. "I don't recall giving you a choice."

Red was moving before anyone could stop him. A blur of fury, he slammed into Black Bullet with a sound like a freight train colliding with a concrete wall. The impact shook the shelves, books spilling like broken teeth onto the floor.

"You'll touch our child over my dead body," Red roared, his fist connecting with Black Bullet's jaw. The strikes were fast, wild and desperate. Black Bullet was forced back, his body crashing against the far wall.

Black Bullet laughed. With bone-snapping precision, he caught Red mid swing, his hand crushing Red's armour with the sound of a smashed can. Red crumpled, his body a limp shadow as he was dragged back up only to be hurled across the desk, wood splintering.

"Pathetic," Black Bullet sneered. "This is the man you trust with your life? The man you made the father of my bloodline? He couldn't protect his first son; what chance does he have with yours?"

Red's armour creaked as he tried to rise, coughing blood, but Black Bullet was on him in a moment, his boot on Red's back, pressing him back down. Sparks flew from Red's damaged suit, the smell of ozone burning the air.

"Medea," I whispered. "Cover me."

Medea didn't argue; in a moment, the room was filled with countless exact replicas of me. I couldn't make them all out, but it was obvious the way they mirrored my movements. The room spun, the move distorting the physics of the study and making it impossible to tell up from down. Mirrors of me crowded the walls and floor, masking the others in the process.

"Are we running?" Road Kill asked.

"Don't even think about it," I warned.

My hands were shaking, but I forced them steady as I reached for my tablet. I took a breath, remembering the feel of Red's hand guiding mine. The rhythm of our fingers on the screen. My fingers found the command, slow, halting, but right. Each click of the keys was a drumbeat in my ears.

"What are you trying to do, Velvet?" Black Bullet laughed, his fists lazily swiping through the illusions one by one. Red's armour groaned in protest, his breath laboured as Black Bullet bore down. "I made sure your connection to the mainframe was shut down permanently."

"The fact," I said, keeping my focus on the screen, "that you thought we wouldn't make copies and compile them into a media bomb, is slightly insulting."

I hit upload and sent Red's custom code into action, sending all the copied files mainframe outward, unchecked, unstoppable. Warning sirens blared from Red's damaged suit. Black Bullet's coms came to life with multiple panicked voices shouting about the leak in the system.

I forced myself to sit taller, though my heart was hammering like a snare drum. "Who's the villain now?"

Black Bullet's composure finally cracked. His voice thundered, all pretense gone. "You're stupid, bitch. You have no idea what you've done!"

His rage hit like heat rolling off a furnace, a shockwave crashed through the room, shattering the illusions and throwing us to the ground. Black Bullet tore his boot away from Red and lunged at me.

I froze, tablet held out uselessly in front of me. Red shouted my name as the menacing shadow closed in.

Glass shattered.

Road Kill snapped forward and struck Black Bullet square in the face. Liquid burst from his palm, splattering across Black Bullet's eyes and mouth, and dripping down his chin. At first, I assumed he was bleeding, until the smell hit me. The acrid scent of Oblivion.

There was a beat where no one moved, the very air frozen around us. Then Black Bullet began to laugh. A humourless, unsettling sound.

"Did you really think—"

Then it hit.

The laughter twisted into a scream. The eerie glow of his eyes, barely a meter away, flickered and dimmed. The hum of power that always seemed to ripple off him, the ozone tang in the air, collapsed like a tower of cards. Black Bullet staggered, clawing at his face, gasping as if his lungs had turned to ash.

"I can handle my power," Road Kill spat. "Let's see how you do without yours."

Black Bullet's knees buckled, his hands scraping against the floor as though searching for something that wasn't there.

"Looks like the king has lost his crown," Medea snarked.

Red dragged himself upright, bloodied and battered. I stumbled over to him, and he clung to me, pressing bloody lips to my brow.

"We need to go," he said. "Now, before backup arrives."

No one was keen to argue. We rushed from the room, leaving Black Bullet behind, exposed, broken and afraid.

Epilogue

The city was in chaos, but that was where villains thrived.

With the data leak, Titan Global's chokehold fractured. The Super Alliance was in disarray, the worship of the masses souring overnight. The remnants of the Twilight Syndicate scattered like rats, with countless villains now free of their leashes, the city had its hands full. For the first time in months, we had space to breathe. Even if the air tasted of ash and broken promises.

With the heat off of us for the moment, Red was able to access his hidden accounts. Dirty money, shell corporations and a few safe-deposit boxes under false identities. We had more than enough to disappear. The Broker, Black Bullet and, even Oblivion, would be behind us, while anything we could imagine lay ahead.

"How long, Blue?" Red asked in the half-light of the empty rail yard where we waited for the others. Our bags were packed and at our feet, the city a hazy blur on the horizon. The smell of creosote and rust thick like a blanket.

"How long?" I repeated, confused.

"How long have you known who I really am?" He asked, his voice careful, like he was defusing a bomb that could go off at any moment.

"Oh," I whispered and smiled at the memory. "Since the first night you brought me dinner. You told me *Blue Velvet* was your favourite song. You told me the same thing when we first met at the hospital when Sam was still alive."

He sighed. "I thought I'd blown it as soon as I said it, but you didn't say anything and I deluded myself into thinking I'd gotten away with it."

"I didn't want to risk never seeing you again," I admitted.

Something eased in him, guilt loosening its hold. "I'm sorry I didn't tell you sooner."

"You didn't have to," I assured him, leaning up for a kiss. "I told you I knew who you were. I still do."

"Save it for the honeymoon!" A voice rang out over the yard. I could make out the three figures approaching, backed by the sunset.

"You're not packed?" Red observed, and I frowned.

"Yeah, we've decided to stay," Nefarious said, crossing to me and pulling me into a tight embrace. I squeezed him back, stunned.

"There are too many kids who need my help," He explained as he pulled away. "Too much hurt I can heal, and with everything going on, the hospitals are liable to be way more lenient of unorthodox methods.”

“I’m staying too,” Road Kill said. “The doc thinks he can help stabilize my powers so the healing won’t take so much out of me. I’ll be able to help people properly.”

“What about Oblivion?” I asked. “You have the formula. You could use it.”

“I burnt it,” Road Kill admitted. “I know I should have asked first, but that much power, it’s not good for anyone.”

I wasn’t mad, but I was worried. “Black Bullet will have it out for you even more now.”

“In the court of public opinion,” Medea proclaimed. “Black Bullet and his minions in the Super Alliance are out. People who help sick kids are in.”

“Don’t tell me you’re staying too,” Red asked her, sounding more than a little crushed.

“Don’t be like that,” Medea told him, walking forward to hold him tight. “I’ll be in touch, and I expect many pictures when the peanut is born, but I have unfinished business with Black Bullet. If he really does know who killed my parents, I owe it to myself to see it through.”

“He could’ve been bluffing,” I pointed out. “He was trying to divide us.”

“Either way, it’s the first lead I’ve gotten in years. If it doesn’t pan out, I’ll come find you and crash on your couch.”

“Oh,” Red said, “goodie!”

She pressed a loud kiss to his cheek and backed away. "By the way, have you picked out a name?"

"Mmmhmm," Red hummed. I could hear the smile return to his voice.

"Blaine," I told them.

"Lovely," Medea crooned. "Classic, strong."

"It means yellow," Red told her, holding back a chuckle.

A beat. "Yellow?" she blurted in disappointment.

Road Kill burst into laughter. "Oh, that's perfect."

"It is not!" Medea protested. "It is akin to child abuse!"

"I wouldn't go that far," Nefarious shrugged. "Come on, these guys need to get going, and so do we."

"I will not forgive you," Medea wagged her long finger inches from my nose before turning to leave.

Road Kill hesitated. "Velvet? Thanks for not giving up on me."

Tears sprang to my eyes, and I rushed forward to hug him tight. "Thanks for putting your faith in me."

He squeezed me back then pulled away, sniffing slightly and turned to go.

Then, it was just us, the sunset a backdrop of an entire future laid out before us. The baby shifted under my ribs, and Red's hand found its way to my stomach, protective and steadying. His thumb brushed circles around my navel that I could feel all the way to my chest.

A faint mosquito hum broke the silence. Too clean, too precise.

"A drone," Red whispered, pulling me into the shadow of a nearby boxcar. I listened to it fly overhead, the buzzing fading away into the distance.

"They're still out there," I whispered.

"Rule number one," Red reminded me.

I turned toward him, finding his chest and pressing both hands flat until I felt his hammering heart. "No," I said softly. "Not anymore. If we're going to build a life together, raise this child, we're going to have to trust each other."

He let the words hang there between us before slowly pulling the scarlet cowl from his head and dropping it with a thud to the ground. His eyes were green, beneath the shadows, his brown hair flattened with sweat.

"Then Red Cypher is dead," he told me. "Though it's not like rule number one ever really applied to us."

I stuck out my hand to him, and he stared at it for a long, confused moment before taking it.

"Hello, Aiden Hall, my name is Velvet Walker. It's good to see you again."

Red let out a bark of laughter and pulled me into his arms. "Hello, Velvet Walker. I've been meaning to tell you, I love you."

He leaned down and kissed me, for the first time without the mask.
We didn't need it anymore.

The End

Jessie Pyne books also published by BWL Publishing Inc.

The Banished World
The Shattered Cage
The Tainted Journey

Even as a young child I would conjure up stories with my imagination, sharing them with anyone who was around to listen. I've developed my storytelling and writing quite a bit since then, but the essence of creativity and entertainment I began with as a kid has remained a major influence on my work.

By day I am an Early Childhood Educator in Saskatoon, Saskatchewan. Working with children ensures that I will never truly have to grow up.